S0-AJJ-156

Palo Alto City Library

The individual borrower is responsible for all library material borrowed on his or her card.

Charges as determined by the CITY OF PALO ALTO will be assessed for each overdue item.

Damaged or non-returned property will be billed to the individual borrower by the CITY OF PALO ALTO.

A TIME
OF FINE
WEATHER

By the same author:

The Poor Old Lady's Dead

The Shallow Grave

A Clutch of Vipers

The Gospel Lamb

The Bastard's Name Was Bristow

An Uprush of Mayhem

The Local Lads

Corporal Smithers, Deceased

All the Pretty People

A TIME
OF FINE
WEATHER

Jack S. Scott

A
Joan
Kahn
BOOK

ST. MARTIN'S PRESS
NEW YORK

A TIME OF FINE WEATHER. Copyright © 1985 by Jack S. Scott. All rights reserved. Printed in the United States of America. No part of this book may be used or reproduced in any manner whatsoever without written permission except in the case of brief quotations embodied in critical articles or reviews. For information, address St. Martin's Press, 175 Fifth Avenue, New York, N.Y. 10010.

Copy Editor: Erika Schmid
Design by Paolo Pepe

A Joan Kahn Book

Library of Congress Cataloging in Publication Data

Scott, Jack S.
   A time of fine weather.

   "A Joan Kahn book."
   I. Title.
PR6069.C589T5 1985   823'.914   85-42
ISBN 0-312-80509-8

First Edition

10 9 8 7 6 5 4 3 2 1

A TIME
OF FINE
WEATHER

1

They had finished making love when Charlie noticed the red flickering glare and heard a fierce crackling. No, not finished entirely, but all the foreplay and frantic progression to glorious release were over, and they were lying clasped in their soft and happy swoon, and when at last Charlie opened his dozy eyes he found the room pulsating with this lurid light. It took a little time for the oddity to register, because the love-lulled mind has jettisoned the tensions from which spring quick reaction and is not surprised that the world this side of the late shattering has been relit. When at last he did absorb, he said, "God Almighty!" and left the bed abruptly, with a scrambling leap.

The unalloyed good remaining in their marriage was what dear old dimpling guidance counsellors call the physical side. Always, to this very day, they could knock each other out, so the distaff partner was not yet down from her pink cloud. Her name was Sally, and they had been married five years. She came down now, abruptly, saying, "What—what—?"

Charlie was at the window, pushing aside the drawn curtains. He could not see the house next door because it stood level with this one, in its identical small but adequate garden, but it was obvious where the pulsating light was coming from. A night-wind gave him a glimpse of flames, too, and there were sparks. "It's Tommy Grover's house," he said. "It's on fire."

"What?" Sally sat up now, with a jerk. "On fire?" And then, bumped all the way back to earth: "Oh my God."

Charlie was on his way to the door, crying as he travelled over carpet recently become their own by virtue of their having kept up the payments to the bitter end. (Only the kitchen to pay for now, and in twenty years the house itself would be theirs. If they got that far.) "Call the fire brigade—the fire brigade!"

"Put something on," she babbled, scrambling her own pretty nakedness out of bed. Woman do not, except in their secret dreams, approve public pube-display. This springs from childhood training and centuries of social pressure. As do the lurid dreams.

Charlie swerved. They loved with the light on, so he fell over nothing as he swooped to where his dressing gown lay, dropped on the floor by the bed. This had not been a night for pyjamas. His were neatly folded still under his pillow, her nightdress equally neat under hers. He did not stay to fumble and hop about on one leg, trying to force feet into trousers that always screwed up when breached in a hurry; but he did don his slippers, stepping straight in while he tugged the dressing gown on, tying the cord as he rushed to the door, crying again, "The fire brigade— ring the bloody fire brigade!"

She was halfway to doing it already, fleeing down the stairs to the hall where the telephone stood. He closed to no more than four treads behind when she got to the bottom, where they diverged, and he was gone through the front door before she had dialled the first nine. Which in her bemused state she did before she picked up the instrument, and so had to start all over again.

Charlie, when he was outside, found the next-door house well away, flames licking out from the front upper windows but the main blaze toward the back. And nobody about. No Grovers, husband or wife or toddling daughter. Tommy's car was not in the drive, but Julie's mini-runabout stood there, outside the garage doors. In this quiet and honest neighbourhood people often left their cars in the drive, and most families owned two. There were lights coming on in one or two of the houses nearby, but he did not notice. His attention was fixed on the blaze.

They must be in there, Julie and small Mandy. They *were* in there: When he came home from work they were coming back

2

from an outing; during the warm June evening they were in the garden, taking advantage, as most people were, of the unusual heat wave. He saw them there—he remembered distinctly fancying Julie, stretched on the grass in her bikini. He saw small Mandy taken in at bedtime; he saw Julie come out again in a short white towelling wrap more fanciable even than the bikini, to sit awhile in a lounging chair until dusk began to creep, and she went in. He had not been watching *all* the time, he wasn't your friendly neighbourhood dirty-raincoat man; but they had to be in there, they wouldn't have gone anywhere.

He slammed the front gate out of his way and rushed up the short drive. Hammered on the door, shouting, "Julie! Julie!" There was no answer, nobody shouted back. More lights were appearing now in the neat detached houses, and a Mr. Fellows who lived opposite shot out of his front gate and came charging across the road. Unseeing, Charlie was putting his shoulder to the door.

Mr. Fellows appeared beside him, saying ridiculously, "What's up? What's up?" It should have been obvious what was up; the bloody house was burning down. Probably he meant, "Who's in there?" Something like that. People react oddly to sudden panic in the night. The man was in pyjamas, frogged down the front. Hadn't even got his teeth in.

"Julie—the baby—" shouted Charlie, and put his shoulder to the door again. But it was a good door, covered by the builder's guarantee.

"Window—window," Mr. Fellows cried, and floundered across a flower bed. Charlie followed. You'd have thought Mr. Fellows did this sort of thing quite often. Even as he trampled the pansies and Canterbury bells he was ripping off his pyjama jacket, wrapping it round his fist. By the time Charlie caught up he had smashed a pane and was fumbling for the interior catch. The window slid up.

Neither man said anything. Mr. Fellows had lost his teeth and a good deal of hair to the merciless years, but judged on current

3

performance not a lot of his youthful agility. It is like being chased by a bull: Whatever your normal condition of health, you can soar over hedges like a swallow. Up and across the windowsill went Mr. Fellows, stuck only for a moment with hands on the floor and his legs still outside, waggling in the air; and without quite knowing he had done it, Charlie found himself also in the room, standing beside him. With one accord they started forward.

It was hot, and choking-smoky, but there were no flames in here. Flame snarled at them when they opened the door. Snarled and crackled hungrily, feeding on the new draught they had made. The heat was intense, reaching for them suddenly; but the fire itself roared upward, from halfway down the stairs, leaping the bottom treads as it belched from the kitchen at the back of the house. Choking in the smoke, Mr. Fellows yelled,

"Can't—get up there—can't—they'll be up there—"

Charlie was on his way: moving forward, mounting the stairs; crouched low, believing he might crawl—under the flames—Julie up there—and the baby— He kicked when his leg was gripped, kicked hard, but Mr. Fellows hung on, pulling him back so that he lost balance and was bumped on his belly down the carpeted stairs. The toothless mouth was crying,

"No—can't—get up—sod it, sod it, sod it." Charlie had never heard him swear before. Admittedly, he did not know him well, but the man was a church warden. And he was yelling on: "Out—never get to—fumes—kill—out—" And then he collapsed.

Now Charlie did the hauling: gripping the ankles, choking—swearing—reeling as the terrible smoke tore his lungs, seared with the sheer heat; back through the room to the window. Somehow he hauled Mr. Fellows upright, as near as his lolling would permit. Somebody else was outside now, the body was going up and out through the window; and Charlie was following, blundering into supporting arms out where the fresh air was—the air—the wonderful cool and beautiful air.

It was all blurring a little for Charlie. Fire engines were shrieking, lights flashed in the road. There were people about now—standing out in front of their houses, moving forward to form a group, some still watching from windows as the firemen leaped off and out of the shuddering engines to unroll hoses, shift ladders, everything lit starkly by the leaping flames.

Sally was there, trying to drape his overcoat across his shoulders. "I don't want it, I don't want it," he snarled, shrugging it away with his eyes fixed on the blazing house where Julie and the baby must be. Three men—neighbours but unfamiliar, quite unrecognizable without the regulation season-ticket-holder office wear or sporty garb of leisure time—had charge of Mr. Fellows, who was sitting up now and appeared to be spewing.

A fireman came over. He spoke politely. "I'm afraid I must ask you folks to stand back—right back—other side of the road."

"There's a woman in there," Charlie said. "And a baby." And Sally added, quite uselessly, "Julie. Julie Grover."

"You won't help them by getting in the way," said the fireman firmly. He spread his arms to shepherd them. "The other side of the road, if you please."

They crossed the road, the human need to huddle in times of calamity bringing them straight to the neighbours who had formed into a group. Nobody said anything; nobody even looked at them. Ordinary people all, who smiled when they said good morning and used New Blue Soko in their washing machines; set-faced now, eyes fixed on the fire, the group and its surroundings rendered theatrical by the melodramatic lighting; watching the firemen being raised up on ladders to direct the force-fed hoses. Watching the roof fall in with a great up-gushing of flame and sparks. Saying—one of them—very softly, "Oh my Christ."

A car came into the street, from the main road end. Tommy Grover's car, the blue Rover. It stopped close by the group, all heads turned now to see it. Tommy came out, running almost before he hit the ground, headed for his front gate. A fireman intercepted him, spoke briefly. Tommy cried—they heard him,

5

quite clearly—"My God—my God!" He tried to run on. The fireman grappled with him, was joined by a sudden policeman, materialised out of somewhere. Together they held him back, tugged
him struggling across to where the group stood. "It's no good,
sir—it's no good," the fireman was saying.

Sally started forward, with Charlie at her elbow. She had
draped the coat over her own dressing-gowned shoulders.
"Tommy—Tommy—" she said.

The policeman looked at her, maintaining his rigid professional
grip. Neither of the other men seemed to hear. Tommy, struggling with face distorted, kept his horror-bolted eyes on his
house. The fireman was speaking again.

"It's no good, sir—nobody can get in there—we've tried—"

And they had. Two firemen had gone in through that open
window, wearing baggy flameproof suits and smoke masks. They
soon came out again.

"My wife—Julie—the baby—" Tommy babbled, fighting. Two
male neighbours were coming forward now, to stand beside Sally
and Charlie. The fireman looked at the policeman. The policeman nodded. The fireman turned in his big boots and crossed
the road again. The policeman said to Tommy, "I'm sorry, sir—
you couldn't do nothing in there."

Sally spoke again. "Tommy—Tommy—"

He stopped struggling and looked at her. "Julie—the baby—"
he said, and snapped into action again, almost breaking from the
policeman's grip. The two male neighbours came close—they
were here in case help was needed to hold him back—and
Charlie with them. They formed a shield with their bodies between Tommy and the blaze; not deliberately to shut it from his
sight but because in front of him was the obvious place to stand,
since that was the way he would run. He fought for a moment
and then suddenly seemed to collapse. Sat down abruptly on the
pavement, gasping and juddering with his hands over his eyes.
The policeman made no move to restrain her when Sally went to
her knees beside him, murmuring half-coherently. Not even

6

when she reached and held him with his head against her shoulder.

By now the fire was dying, smashed and smothered by those formidable hoses. There was more steam now than smoke.

By three o'clock in the morning it was all over. One red engine remained in the street still, hoses ready and crew poking among the steaming ruin of the gutted house, making sure that nothing remained to flare up again. A police car stood nearby, so the original helmeted police presence had been augmented by two chequed-capped constables. Not much for them to do, no crowds to hold back. A few groups only, come in from surrounding streets; all docile enough, giving no trouble. Some of the neighbours were out there still, but most had gone back into their houses. Not to bed, though, every one was showing lights. The bodies of Julie and the baby had been taken away in an ambulance that slid into the street and out again, ten minutes ago. None of the watchers saw them, they were covered over with blankets.

Tommy did not see them. He was with Charlie and Sally in their living room. They took him into the house—he did not resist, all the resistance seemed to have gone out of him—after that leading fireman came across to where he sat, still with Sally's arms about him and his face buried, to shrug and spread his arms; to shake his head, putting the message across silently; murmuring low to Charlie, whose connection with Sally was obvious since he stood so close beside her, "Can you get him away from here?"

They coaxed him to his feet then and he came with them, Sally's arm still about him, Charlie's hand on his shoulder. There was whisky in the house, there was a little gin, there was vodka; but they gave him the drop of brandy left over from Christmas. People always give brandy at times of appalling shock. It does no more, probably, than whisky or gin or vodka would; but in the ministering mind, shock and brandy go together.

He did not drink it. He accepted the glass and sat huddled on their settee, a squarish, not tall but rather good-looking man who couldn't be far from forty, drawing great, shuddering breaths from time to time and gazing glassy-eyed into space, holding the glass between his spread knees. Very good suit he was wearing. They go for good suits in high-mortgage areas.

The policemen from the squad car came in, and a doctor who must have arrived with the ambulance. The policemen asked quiet questions: names and the address—that seemed a bit super-fluous, they should have known what street they were in and there were numbers and/or names on all the front gates—and the doctor, low-voiced after a glance at him, said he would send a nurse with a car to bring him down to the hospital, where an eye could be kept on him. Observation, he called it. Tommy sat nurs-ing his glass and drawing those juddering, rasping breaths, taking no notice of any of them.

They sent a small, low vehicle not very different from a station wagon, painted white and with AMBULANCE spelled out along the sides. Two men in white coats came with it. Tommy went with them, still blanked out and leaving the brandy untasted. When he was gone and they came back in after brushing off Mrs. Bradleigh, who bustled across to tap the meaty-heart of sensation as she will bustle to whoever is left after they drop the bomb, Charlie said, naked under his dressing gown,

"Want a drink?"

"I—" said Sally. "I—yes. No. No, I don't think so." She was fully dressed.

"I do, by Christ," Charlie said. He crossed to the sideboard, where the bottle stood, to pour himself the stiffest kind of whisky. He could have had the brandy, but somehow it was now taboo. All they had went into that glass, and later they poured it down the sink. He took a great gulp; topped up, almost to the brim. When he turned round she was weeping silently, the tears coursing down her unmade-up face.

He left the glass where it stood and moved swiftly, folding her into his arms. "There, there," he murmured. "There, there—come on now—come on now—"

She groaned. Literally groaned, her face buried into his chest, hands dug into his back, all her body shaking. "Oh—oh—oh Christ—oh—oh—"

2

Charlie had expected that they would sit up for what was left of the time before the ringing of alarm clocks. It was, after all, four o'clock on a June morning, there was dawn in the sky. But after a while he felt Sally's sudden surging need, felt his male body stiffen almost with a jolt as her lips came up moaning to seek his, all her urgent face salty and wet with tears.

So he took her up to bed and they came together as though they were only in minor degree physical—a sobbing, obliterating spirit-naked time of release from overwhelming shock. The too-stressed mind, saving itself. And then they slept, clinging together like worn-out children. Not until seven o'clock did Sally open her eyes, and think, Oh damn—I should have rung the paper.

She slipped out of bed, Charlie sleeping still, and went down to the hall. Her editor was not yet in, of course, and wouldn't be for a couple of hours. It was the night-desk man who said, "Morning. *Evening Courier.*"

She told of the fire. The voice sounded less than pleased. "Bit bloody late, aren't you? We had it hours ago—Georgie Baynes covered it. Christ, girlie—right next bloody door? And you didn't even ring? Not the first night of your honeymoon, is it?"

"Get knotted," she said, and slammed the phone down. Stuff him—she'd explain to Harry, later. He'd lecture a bit—a reporter has two duties: to the paper and to the public—but he would understand.

What the hell did it matter, anyway? What there was to gather

10

would have been garnered by Georgie Baynes. There was no early morning deadline, they served the town as an evening paper. And anyway, by rights she was a feature writer. Reporter when necessary, yes, all smallish-town journalists are; but officially, feature writer. Own byline and everything, her bi-weekly column angled for women. Which did not stop the odd dirty letter coming into the office from anonymous men attracted by her picture. Strange, the things they wanted to do to her. Even stranger, the things they wanted her to do to them.

She went from the hall into her bright kitchen, where she filled the kettle and switched it on. Then she mounted the stairs again to see if Charlie was awake and wanting a cup.

His eyes were open. He was lying on his back with his hands behind his head. No fat on him at thirty-five, he insured against it by playing a lot of squash, with cricket in its season. Who should insure better than the man who lives by insurance? He said, "Good morning, Miss Pennard." Pronouncing it, as usual when the light corniness of affection was proper between them— not so often, nowadays—with exaggerated emphasis on the last syllable, the way the snobbier of her relatives did without humourous intent. She was Pennard before marriage made Wood out of her. Not everybody knew she was Wood, professionally she had carried on using her maiden name. Her byline still said Sally Pennard.

"Want a cuppa?" she asked.

"Wouldn't mind." He stretched widely, still slack from their loving. "Anything happening next door?"

"I don't know. Didn't look. Kettle's on; do you want it up here?"

"Mm—I've had one helluva night." And as she turned away: "No. No—I'll come down, ring the hospital. See how poor old Tommy is."

"Bit early, isn't it?"

"Get the night staff up off their bums." She was at the door. He called "oy"; and when she looked back, grinned his wide grin

11

at her. The first since before the fire. "Twice in a night. Put that in your column, tell your old ladies how it feels." To him, in the good times when he teased, all her readers were little old ladies. "Twice isn't much," she said. "I can remember when." "Like that it is."

She went back down the stairs to make the tea. While she gathered cups and saucers, biscuits, sugar, milk, and all and stirred the pot to help the brewing, she listened to Charlie, ringing the hospital from the hall. No long conversation, he was in the kitchen by the time she had two cups poured, sugared, and milked, and the lid off the biscuit tin. "How is he?" she said.

"All right. Just shock, he'll be out today. Which is mine? Ta." He picked up his tea and a biscuit, to be dunked. She used to find it endearing, the way he took two sips and then began to dunk his biscuit. Of late, it had irritated her. Not today, though. She had bigger things on her mind. "Where's he going to?" she said.

"I don't know. Relatives?"

"Has he got any?"

"I expect so. Somewhere. Most people have."

People in bed, after good vibrating, enjoy a relaxed insulation from what lies beyond the half-doze, and the more stressed they have been the greater reluctance is in them to let it go. But once they are up . . . "I can't help thinking of Julie and—the baby," said Sally. "It's—oh—it's—horrible."

"Yes," Charlie said. "Yes. Terrible. Can't believe it, it just— You can't sort of take it in."

"It must have started while we were . . . We're all so bloody self-centred. We didn't even know." The tears were in her eyes again. Women are luckier than men in this; society permits them the relief that lies in weeping.

"We're human, that's all. We're not made to think about the people next door while we're at it. Although some do, they tell me." I have, in my time. I've wondered what it would be like, while I was making it with you, to be doing it with Julie. Christ—it's horrible. It's bloody horrible.

12

"Don't philosophize at me, for God's sake. And don't be flippant about it."

He wasn't being flippant. Not for the fun of it. But there are things too ghastly to be spoken of in any serious way. She was in the garden only yesterday evening. In a bikini, beautiful body creamy-skinned and alive. She was part of the build-up to his first need, the first bout with Sally; and while they were actually engaged, that creamy body—and the bab . . . Oh Christ—Christ—it was horrible.

"What do you want for breakfast?" Sally asked. The gay yellowy curtains were still closed across the window. Neither had moved to draw them back. From here, until you stepped through the back door, the destroyed house could not be seen. But the garden could, with Julie's lounger and the rubber duck little Mandy used to float in the blow-up paddling pool. The pool itself was out there, blue with yellow ducks around the rim.

"I don't think I want any," he said. "Not very hungry. I'll just—have a bath, I think. And another cup of tea."

Earlier up than usual and with no time needed for eating breakfast, he was able to bath leisurely where normally he stood briefly under the shower, and to linger over shaving and tooth-cleaning and dressing as usually he could do only at week-ends. The fact brought him no pleasure. He wanted to be at work, away from here for a while. He wondered if Sally felt the same, whether she would stay to work—it was one of her column-writing days, she always did it at home—or retreat to the office.

He asked her, just before he left. "I don't know," she said. "Probably stay. They'll all be talking about it, at the office."

"Wonder how old Fellows is feeling? Poor old bugger, he flaked right out. Gutty, though."

"You'll probably both find yourselves heroes."

"We didn't do anything."

"Old Harry'll blow it up."

"You going to tell him?"

"Well—I'll have to, won't I? If I don't, somebody else will. I'm surprised he hasn't been on." The phone rang. "Bet that's him now."

"Tell him I've gone," he said, and left the house as she was saying, "Ah—good morning, Harry. Yes—yes—it was quite a thing. . . ."

One fire appliance stood still in the road outside, together with a black-and-white police car. One policeman guarded the gate to the black ruin of Tommy's nice home and several men in plain clothes were grouped within, but he did not stop or stare. He drove away.

It was not far from the town to the city, where his office was. He commuted every day. A happy drive in fine weather, through good country marred at both ends by the inevitable spread of housing-estate suburbs. The five miles left unmolested looked lovely on this heat-wave morning. He drove all the way with the sun-roof open and the windows wound down. Took in a deal of carbon monoxide as he weaved through the city streets, but urban lungs are inured to that. It caused no pain.

For almost the first time in his business career—the other time was on his first nervous morning—he arrived before the office was open. The main part of the ground floor was a-clack with typing, all the girls ranked at desks along the open hall, but nobody above the level of dogbody-clerk or copy-typist starts work, in insurance, before ten o'clock. It is status confirmation, to be the one graciously acknowledging the chorus of good-mornings as you pass through rather than one commanded to be here at nine-thirty, ready to speak the chorus.

He went for coffee to a nearby café much favoured by middle-echelon, and glanced through his daily paper. Too much to say that he read it, *The Times* does not yield all its secrets over one cup of coffee; but he did find that in this paper, anyway, there was no mention of the fire. Not a big story, by national newspaper standards, in spite of two deaths. Later editions might carry it, but it was not used in this one.

At ten o'clock he went to his office, walking through the typewriter-chattering hall, smiling his nice smile as he replied to the morning greetings. Most of the girls were pretty, many of them—say most of them, he was a normal male—he fancied. Some quite obviously fancied him. They smiled the widest, spoke most little-girlishly, and when he was gone from sight dropped their pretty eyes back to the keys and drifted him into whatever fantasies they wove to help them through their daily incarceration.

His desk was one of two in a bright, pleasant office. There was carpet on the floor, slat blinds at the windows, a rubber plant in a Mexican-looking pot, and jazzy abstract prints on linen-papered walls. He shared it with one Benny Greenslade, and leading off from it was a smaller, even deeper-carpeted office with a genuine Wilson Steer and a believed-to-be Old Crome in place of the jazzy abstracts. Herein dwelt his immediate boss, Bert Porter, who did not design the décor.

The door between the rooms was standing open. As he entered, a high tenor voice floated out from within. "That you, Charlie?"

"Morning, Bert," he called. "In already?"

"Come in here, will you?"

Charlie stepped through, onto the thicker carpet. The man who occupied this little room was not cut to match it. He was a slob, big and fat and untidy, with hair too long at the back, combed carefully over to disguise baldness. A chain-smoker, a man with bottles locked away in one drawer of the expensive desk. Not the man you would choose to take with you for tea with the Archbishop of Canterbury. A good investigator, though, with a sharp nose for fraud. Charlie had learned a lot from him since he joined this small investigating team a year ago, after an abortive period of selling. He sat now as ever, overflowing the leather swivel chair with the inevitable cigarette stuck to his thick lower lip, ash all down his waistcoat. He fluted, as Charlie entered,

"You had a fire, down your way."

"Too bloody true, we did. Right next door."

"Mate of yours." A statement, not a question.

15

"Yes. Tommy Grover."

"You'd better have it, then. You'll have to anyway; Benny's got a couple of car crashes."

"What do you mean, have it?"

"Fuzz's just been on. Another mate of yours, Pete Parsons. Reckons somebody shoved something through the cat-flap at the back."

"Arson?" It is literal truth: At moments of severe shock, the blood is suddenly chilled and hair upon the nape of the neck rises.

"Well—looks like it. Dunn it? And we carry the insurance. Don't we? You ought to know, you sold him the bloody policy."

An insurance man at news of calamity thinks automatically about the insurance. Charlie had, with relation to the fire; but only in passing, more serious aspects had crowded his mind. "His wife was killed," he said, "and his little girl."

"I know. Bastard, annit? You'd better get over there. And don't hang about; if they're farting around with the bits and pieces, I want somebody on the spot."

3

Charlie rang Sally before he set out again along that pleasant road to home. He said: "Sal, listen—are there people still poking around next door?"

"I don't know." She was keeping the kitchen curtains drawn, and the living room, where she had set up typewriter and the other tools of her trade, ready for when she could concentrate, did not overlook the neighbouring ruin. "I haven't been out."

"Well, if there are, one of 'em will be old Pete Parsons. He'll probably have a fire bloke with him, could be Tony Scully. Tell him I'm on the way, eh?"

"On the way? Why?"

"Somebody might have chucked a bomber in. Through the cat door."

"No. Oh no—oh no!"

"That's what Bert Porter reckons. Says Pete rang him."

"But—oh no—"

"Look, love—just tell Pete I'm on it, and on my way. If he's finished before I get there, give him a cup of tea or something. Right? And listen—don't ring your bloody rag. All right?"

Half an hour later—it takes that long to cover eight miles, starting from the city traffic—he drew into his drive. The fire engine was gone from the street, but parked there now were the police car, the blue family saloon belonging to Detective Chief Inspector Pete Parsons, and an estate-car-type van, one of those used by fire officers when they oversee operations. If that came with Tony, Charlie thought, half the bloody cricket club's here.

But for the ruin next door, the world beamed today as the sun built up the gratifying heat. There were palely ginger people with blood made skinny by evolution from dank, primeval swamp glooming under grey and weeping skies who moaned that it was too hot; but the country in general stripped off woolly underwear and happily carried its jacket over its arm. In gardens, including Charlie's, the flowers luxuriated. He had not put them there himself. Sally hoed and weeded a little, but most of the work was done by old Bob Hogge, who tended many of the gardens round about. Used to work for the Parks Department.

Normally, Charlie liked his walks from car to front door, he enjoyed the flowers and the general well-groomed ambiance, which he, until he met Sally, never believed he would win and never really aspired to. But today there was no pleasure in it. He passed quickly across to the front door, feeling for his key as he went. A quick glance told him that there was nobody now in the garden next door. Pete and Tony, if it was Tony, would be in his house.

They were—drinking tea in the sun-bright living room. The chunky CID man in one of the Swedish armchairs, his sports coat draped across the back; the fireman in the other, done up to the neck in uniform bearing Divisional Officer insignia. Tall, gangling, a fast bowler with a near-comic whirling action, he was the only man Charlie knew who made him and his six feet feel stunted. Even seated in the low chair he looked tall, and his great hands threatened disaster to Sally's bone china.

"Hi, Pete," said Charlie. "Hallo, Tony. What's all this, then?"

"Didn't they tell you," the detective said, "at the office?"

"Reckoned it was a bomber."

"Petrol. In a jar, or something. Somebody stuck it through the cat-flap. Tony spotted it, gave us a buzz."

The fireman spoke. "Found glass where there shouldn't be any. Melted pretty well, but glass all right. And the cat-flap had been propped up—the bottom of the door didn't burn, they'd used a bit of metal. Made a good draught. Started it off right."

"Ta," said Charlie. Sally had fetched him a cup of tea from the tray on the table. He waved away the biscuits, not even looking at her. No reason why he should, of course, they'd been married five years. "You sure?"

"Still waiting for the forensic report," the policeman told him, "but there's not much doubt about it."

"There's *no* doubt about it," said Tony Scully.

"But—Christ—who'd do—? Why?" He was stirring the tea absently, grating the spoon against the bottom of the cup. Another of his habits that had come to irritate Sally, of late. Today, she did not notice.

"They sent me here to start finding out," said Pete Parsons. Younger than Charlie by two years—and thirty-three is young, for a detective chief inspector—his chunky, solid build made him seem the older; especially when, as now, his smile was missing. "I asked for the job. Did you?"

"I didn't have to, I was the man in line." But, Charlie's mind said, I would have done. Had no chance to even think about it, but now that you ask: "I would have done, if old Bert hadn't put me on it. Have you spoken to Tommy?"

"I was waiting for you. Thought we'd go and have a look at him together. I've been on to the hospital, they say it'll be all right."

"Yes. Right. I'd have been going in to see him, anyway."

"*We'd* have been going in to see him," Sally put in, quietly.

"Yes—well—*we'd* have been going in to see him. Poor old Tom—bloody arson? Who the hell would want to do it?"

"More than arson," said the Chief Inspector. He was rising from his chair. Tony Scully was getting up, too, elongating alarmingly. "It's murder. Double murder."

"Oh Christ," Charlie said. "Yes. Yes."

"Manslaughter at the very least. Ready, then? Thanks for the tea, Sal. Lovely."

"Yes—ta, Sal," said Tony Scully. "Great."

She hated being called Sal. That didn't stop people doing it.

19

She asked the policeman the necessary question. "Can I ring the office, let Harry in on it?"

"Not yet, love—wait 'til I get the forensic report, huh? I'll ring you as soon as it's through. Once it's more than fishy, we'll want all the publicity we can get. Billy the Fumer'll be guv'nor, but he knows I want it." They all knew who Billy the Fumer was. Detective Chief Superintendent William Henry Fumery, the records called him. He earned the nickname, being a man given to fuming when things got on top of him. Given this and a name like his, it had to happen.

"Yes. All right," Sally said.

They said good-by to her, and left. Outside in the road they paused before separating. Tony said, "Well, that lets me out. I'll get back and do the Home Office report. I'll send copies of the photos round, Pete. They're not going to be pretty." One of the tasks of the Fire Brigade after a fire is to take pictures showing the bodies, if any, their position in the room, and so on.

"Yes—all right, mate. Ta." The police would have their own photographs, but annotated Fire Brigade ones cannot fail to be useful.

"See you Saturday? I've got Tommy down to play, too, but I don't suppose he'll be keen." The tall man was captain of the cricket team to which they all belonged.

"Don't suppose he will," said the policeman. "Poor old bugger. Me—it'll be subject to the exigencies of the service."

"Always bloody is," Tony said. "You're never bloody there when you're wanted. Julie was down to do the teas. Bastard, ain't it? Well—give old Tommy my—you know. See you." He turned away, to fold himself into his van. Charlie moved on with Pete, to the blue saloon.

They did not talk much on the way to the hospital. When a thing like this has happened to friends, light chat does not spring easy to the lips. And these were two professionals now, each busy with his own thinking. No need to entertain each other. Never had been, in all the years since they joined the force and walked the beat together.

Ten years Charlie was a policeman. But he lacked Pete Parsons' unstoppable flair. He stuck as though Bosticked to the bottom rung while his mate ran happily up the ladder. Four years ago he resigned and took to insurance, where the rewards are bigger and come quicker. Inevitably, with his police background, he had come by Bert Porter's inveigling into the investigation department, where he found his own flair, and was paid even more. His old contacts were very useful, and his friendship with Pete carried straight on, partly because of cricket.

They had worked together only once in the years—this silly man burned his shop out and left a trail of tapers right across from the door, over the counter, and on to his most combustible stock. But every week in season they batted together, sank the after-match pint together, and generally enjoyed each other; and out of season there were dances and dinners and dinner-dances and indoor practise sessions, at all of which would be Tony Scully and Tommy Grover; and at the social functions, their wives. Who also took their turn with the wives of other members, tea-making and sandwich-serving at the matches, the children toddling around the pavilion to be petted by the teams at tea. Very much a family affair, a happy cricket club.

A ten-minute drive, to the hospital. They found Tommy in a visitor's lounge, dressed in the suit he was wearing last night, all ready to leave. He looked pale and sick; and when they managed to mumble some sort of condolences, he said,

"They passed your message on from the switchboard here, Pete. I thought I'd better wait for you."

"Ah," said the policeman. "Yeah. Good. There's a sort of— complication."

"Complication?"

"Yes. Tony Scully was on the—er—the fire. He gave me a

21

buzz. Seems as if some bastard shoved a starter in through your cat-flap."

Tommy's white skin took on, quite suddenly, a greenish tinge. Brows sprung up, eyes wide, he jerked. "Starter?"

"Arson, mate," said Charlie. "It looks like arson."

"I don't—nobody—who would—?" And Tommy sank to the floor.

They picked him up, still without need for speech—they'd dealt with enough recumbent customers between them, God knows—and laid him on the settee where visitors sit clutching grapes and bunches of flowers. Before they had his tie properly loosened he was stirring. Before they had his pulse felt he was struggling upright, babbling, "What?—What?—What? What happened?"

"You flaked out, me old son," Charlie told him.

"Oh. Did I? I was— Sorry." Tommy sat blinking vaguely at them, still wearing the greenish pallor.

Silence for a moment. Then Pete said, "Well—we won't bother you now. But I'll have to ask you a few questions. Later, when you feel up to it."

"Yes. Yes. All right," said Tommy.

Charlie spoke. "Where are you going from here, Tom?"

"Going?"

"Mm. I mean—where are you going to—you know—live?" Cricketing, drinking, bridge-partying friends know something of each other's backgrounds. There were no relatives handy for Tommy to move in with. Julie had parents, in Chester. But Chester was a long way off, and he would be needed here. He couldn't simply pack a bag and leave it all. What had he got to pack, anyway? The clothes he was not wearing, all his bits and pieces, went up in the fire.

"Oh. I—" Obviously, his mind had not travelled this far. "I'll—get a room. Hotel somewhere."

He can't do that, poor old bugger, Charlie thought. What, sit about in a chilly hotel room, all on his own? Look at him—he'd

22

go round the twist. Somebody'll have to be with him, see he gets his laundry done, see he eats, get him a few shirts and things. "How about coming in with us?" he said. "You know—just 'til you get yourself—well—sorted out a bit."

Clearly, if the matter registered at all with Tommy, it dissolved into blank indifference. "All right," he said. His eyes were fixed on a point straight ahead.

Charlie looked around. "Is there a blower handy? I'd better give Sally a ring."

"One just outside," Pete told him.

"Hang on a minute."

The phone in the passage was attached to the wall, under a plastic bubble cut away to permit ingress. Charlie inserted his head and shoulders, dialled, got a *bzz-bzz-bzz* followed by a *whoop-whoop-whoop* and sent money thunking and clattering into the bowels of the machine. "Sally?" he said. "It's me. Look—I'm at the hospital. I've told old Tom he'd better move in with us for a few days."

"Oh," she said, and there was a short, very short silence.

The strain was telling on him. He felt quick anger flaring. She couldn't object—where the hell else could poor old Tommy go? "Where else can he go? There's no family handy."

She spoke swiftly, catching the truculence in his tone. Matching it, almost. Truculence breeds truculence. "It's not that—it's just that—well, it's right next door, isn't it. It'll be jammed under his nose all the time."

"Well, we can't bloody move, can we? What else could I do?"

"What about Pete, don't they have room?"

"It's got nothing to do with Pete."

"Don't snap," she snapped. "Of course he can come. How long are you going to be?"

"We're leaving now, Pete's still with us."

"I'll get the bed aired." And she hung up.

Back went Charlie to the visitor's lounge. "All right," he said.

23

"Let's go then, huh?" Presumably, it was all right to walk out just like that. No hospital staff appeared to forbid it.

When they had delivered Tommy into Sally's care, they went their separate ways: Pete not very far—into the garden next door, where he joined several other men who were standing in a group watching some uniform constables gathering bits of wreckage into plastic bags, round where the back door used to be—and Charlie back to his office. He reported immediately to the room of his big fat boss, who spoke before he did.

"How'd it go, then?"

"Looks as if it was a bomber, all right. Pete Parsons is going to call me, soon as he gets the official forensic report."

"Don't pay out, then, do we?"

"No. I suppose not. Not yet." Insurance companies suspend such payment automatically, while they wait upon the police. They react to police findings or, if the case goes further, to legal verdicts. It is not their policy to pay out money in circumstances bent, but nobody knowing which way. It is not their policy to pay out money at all, if they can possibly help it.

"If we do pay out," said the fat man.

"What do you mean?"

"Well—you know—never can be sure, can you? Sorted out a lot of fires in my time. Especially around quarter day."

I ought to smash your bloody teeth in, Charlie said in his quick-erupting mind. Aloud, he spoke icily. "He's a mate of mine. He lost his wife and child in it."

"Yeah. Yeah," said fat Bert Porter. "Sorry I spoke, I'm sure." He took the cigarette out of his mouth long enough to flick a length of ash onto the expensive carpet. The cleaning ladies who came in every morning hated him for it. "Well—nothing more we can do for now. Let me have the report on the Davidson lark soon as you can."

Charlie went back to his own office. Took out his ballpoint and hand-wrote his report on the car that killed a John Patrick David-

24

son. Nothing funny about it, simple fracture of a brake pipe. The claim would be met, this report cleared the way for it. When it was done he took it through to the outer office and gave it to a girl who always blushed when he bent over her. "Soon as you can, sweetheart," he said. "Old Fatso's hollering for it."

"Yes, Mr. Wood," she said, blushing and simpering. "Soon's I finish this."

"That's a good girl." He could hear the telephone ringing in his office. "I'll buy you a Guinness at Christmas."

Her blush deepened. She even giggled. "It's a long way to Christmas."

"So try not to get thirsty." He turned away. Thirsty? she thought, watching him go from under her stuck-on lashes. Hungry's what I am.

Back at his desk, Charlie picked up the phone. It spoke in the voice of Detective Chief Inspector Pete Parsons, ringing from the station. He said, "I've got the forensic report here. Take it as official. Petrol, some sort of glass container. We're treating it from here as murder."

"Uh-huh."

"I'll need to see Tommy. Can I call in this evening?"

"Yes. Yes—we'll be there." Tommy, certainly, would not be wanting to gad about.

"I've got men on house-to-house, of course, but I've told 'em to give you a miss. I'd sooner do it myself. Seven o'clock all right?"

"Yes. Sure."

"See you later, then." The phone went dead. Charlie called to the inner office:

"That was Pete Parsons. It's official—petrol bomb."

"Didn't doubt it," fluted his boss. "Let's be having the report, then."

The rest of the day was dull routine. At five o'clock Charlie left the huge concrete-and-tinted-glass building erected by the company out of premium monies. A dollar here, a dollar there, it

25

soon mounts up. By half past five he was driving down his road, noting three teams of men still working. These, his experience knew, were back-up to the earlier house-to-house men. By routine, every house would be knocked upon twice. People often remember a little something between the calls. These second teams would just be starting, to cover the time when workers not yet spoken to would be coming home from the office. Plain-clothed they were, and young, and scruffy, in jeans and sweatshirts or sports vests, because of the heat-wave. A tiring duty, working on the knocker in hot weather. Altogether evil, in snow.

He used his key, and Sally met him in the hall. She'd had a stressful day. With Tommy sitting in deep silence on the settee, it was not easy to concentrate three yards away upon the chattily trivial column, and quite impossible to type it. Too loud, the chattering of the typewriter. She gave up and dictated it over the phone to Marge, who was more or less her secretary. But only on column days, for the rest of the week she belonged to Harry Vincent, Editor. That's how he signed his letters.

She had wondered what to do about lunch. Tommy said he didn't want anything, and she was not hungry. Nevertheless she made Welsh rarebit as something light but solid enough to put a little substance in the belly, keeping the kitchen curtains drawn because there was nothing out there she wanted to see, and nothing, for sure, that he would enjoy should he wander in. As he might, he wasn't chained to the settee. Mind you, he did not move from it all the day through. Not even to go to the toilet.

Pete rang from the police station, as promised, to tell her that the forensic reports were positive, and she phoned the news on to the paper; using the upstairs extension phone and speaking softly. Not that he could hear from where he sat hunched and silent, but it felt like a sort of ghoulish treachery to be doing it at all.

The afternoon was even more difficult. She filled it with housework, repeating small tasks over and over again, to stay out of his way. And nothing much needed doing in the first place; she had a lady who came in three mornings a week. Yesterday was one of her days.

By the time Charlie appeared she was tight with nervous strain, locked into exhaustion and woozy with aspirin. Like many women, she leaned upon aspirin in the hour of need. She said brightly to the still huddled Tommy, "Ah—here comes Charlie," and through her head as she went out to the hall ran a ludicrous refrain she often used to warble as lovey-dovey greeting, in the days when they were so young, and very silly. And very happy. "Clap hands—here comes Charlie—clap hands—good old Charlie. . . ." Her mother started her on it. Sang it when he knocked on the door, come courting.

"Hallo," Charlie said, very softly, as though grave sickness were in the house. "How is he?"

She found herself whispering back. "Hasn't said anything all day. He's just sitting there."

"Where?"

"On the settee." Where do you think, on the loo?

"Uh-huh." He hadn't kissed her. "Pete's coming in to see him. About seven."

"I know. He rang."

"Uh-huh." They moved toward the living room. En route, he arranged his face, to greet the huddled man with bonhomie too loud, too cheery even in his own ears. "Hi, Tom. How's it going, son?"

Tommy looked up, making a brave attempt at this bonhomous bantering tone used by the cricketers when they met. He even managed a smile. It distorted his lips without touching the eyes. "Hi, Charlie. All right, mate. How's yourself?"

"Buggered," said Charlie. "They're roasting cats on the pavement in the city. Anybody need a drink?"

"I do," Sally said promptly. She'd needed one for a long time; but when she offered to Tommy earlier, he turned it down, and she did not like to go it alone.

27

"How about you, mate?" Too loud, too happy-happy. Tone it down, for God's sake.

"All right," said Tommy.

Charlie found himself rubbing his hands. Actually rubbing his hands; but for the heat-sweat they'd have sounded like sandpaper. And when he stopped it, too quickly, he did not know what to do with them. So he crossed to the sideboard and used them for tipping liquids into glasses. Scotch for himself and Tommy, gin always, at this time, for Sally. Topped his with ice and water, topped hers with tonic, and said, "Anything in it, Tom?"

"No," said Tommy. "Thanks."

"Spoken like a Scotchman," said Charlie, fetching the drinks over. Now we're getting facetious, thought Sally. And now, if I know my man, we say down the hatch and jolly good luck. "Down the hatch and jolly good luck," said Charlie.

So it went on. Terribly difficult. When Charlie succeeded in toning down the travelling-salesman cheeriness, he found himself without a lot to say. Sally did not help—she turned the whole thing over to him and retired to the kitchen, to prepare dinner. Tommy roused himself a little now, but what was there to talk about, other than the fire? Charlie's attempts to engage other subjects—last Saturday's match, next Saturday's match, the state of the gardens if normal rain was not restored to them soon— sounded exactly like what they were: deliberate and clumsy angling away from the subject not to be approached. Very, very difficult.

He could not even watch the television news, as he normally did. Halfway to the set he realized that the TV cameras might well have been around today. If they had not, there might be verbal mention. He veered away to the bottles, to mix himself another drink. And one for Tommy.

Then the *Evening Courier* came, flopping through the letter box onto the mat. Sally's paper. He could not go to fetch it; without any doubt at all it would be black with headlines and stuck all

28

over with pictures. It lay in the hall until Sally emerged silently, to bear it away to the kitchen.

They could not go into the garden, even.

And Pete was half an hour late. When Charlie let him in he said, "Sorry, cock. Been sweeping up every little bug who ever lit a firework. How's the boy?"

"Bit umpty," Charlie told him. "He's in the living room."

They went through. Sally was in there now, waiting for the *ping* of the cooker to announce triumphantly yet another dinner done to a turn. Unable to stretch out as usual on the settee with her feet up, she sat pretending to be easy in one of the armchairs. The policeman greeted her. She said, "Hi, Pete. Staying to eat?"

"No, Sal, ta," he said. "Can't spare the time. Well now, young Tom—how are we doing?" His manner was an abridged edition of the salesman bonhomie only recently shaken off by Charlie.

"Fine. Fine," said Tommy, clearly lying. When he smiled his teeth were excellent for a man who must have been knocking on forty.

"Good," said Chief Inspector Parsons. He looked very spruce in his dark suit. Chunky, but spruce. And a lot taller than the burly build promised, when it came up close. More fitted to the area than the scruffy young coppers still working outside. But then, he did not need to get lost among the junkies and layabouts. "All right if I ask a few questions?"

"Yes. Sure," said Tommy.

There were not, in fact, many questions to be asked. The principle one was obvious: Did Tommy know of anybody who would want to do a thing like that?

He said no. No, he didn't. Answering quite calmly, seemingly well under control. The policeman passed on.

No business enemies? No traumatic run-in with a rival or rivals? The restaurant? The haulage firm?

No. No, Tommy did not recall any trouble with business rivals. Only— a month or so ago he refused to pay protection.

29

The policeman's eyes clicked to new focus. "Protection? Who was after protection?"

"I don't know," Tommy said. "Three lads came in. Told me I'd be paying weekly if I didn't want the windows smashed, customers molested."

"At the restaurant?"

"Yes."

"Did you report it?" Pete asked; knowing that he had not, because it would have been circulated at the station. And not only that: friends of a ranking policeman, reporting a thing like this, ask for him by name and tip it into his personal ear. Sillier ones have been known to do it to enlist his aid in a campaign against a hated traffic warden.

"No. I didn't take it seriously. They were three tearaways, that's all. Young lads. Scruffy. Trying it on." Longest speech he had made since he arrived.

To Charlie and Sally, it was obvious that Pete was smothering sharpness in deference to Tommy's condition and the general situation. Even so, something of official crispness coloured his voice when he said, "Can you give me a description?"

"I didn't study them all that closely. Jeans and leather-type jackets. Studs in them. One tall, the others short. Mario and Hans were there, they got rid of them." Mario was his restaurant manager, a Neapolitan probably a lot tougher than his urbanity suggested. Hans drove one of his trucks by day, moonlighting by night as waiter. Did it very well, weaving delicately between the small tables set with coloured candles in bottles. Surprising, considering that he was once a heavyweight boxer of repute in his native Germany, built like a brick model of the Brandenburg Gate. Good man for getting rid of people. Every restaurant open late needs its muscular pacifier. Even the expensive ones. And feeding at Tommy's Belle Epoque did not come cheap.

"Well, that's nice," said Pete. "You can't just let things like that go by."

"We could handle it."

"What about the people who can't?"

"They weren't real hard cases. Just three tearaways, trying it on."

"Even so, we ought to be told. How are we to nobble these little buggers if we don't know about 'em?"

"Sorry." Tommy dropped the word, not really in apology, but to cut off discussion of a point seemingly holding no interest for him. It would take more than this to stand up as rival to his stunned preoccupations. His entire attitude said so.

"Well—if they try it again somewhere, no doubt we'll hear about it," Pete said. He had reached the end of his questioning. There was nothing left to ask. He rose from the chair he sat on. "I'll be on my way."

"Drink before you go?" said Charlie.

"No, thanks. Work to do. See you at the match? That's if I can make it."

"Yes. I expect so. Show the gentleman the door, woman."

"Evening, all," said Pete, touching his forehead in the traditional policeman parody.

Five minutes later the cooker went *ping*. Sally got up to attend to it. Tommy said, "Do you mind if I use your phone?"

"Help yourself," said Charlie. "You know where it is."

"Better just let Mario know I won't be in tonight." Tommy rose from the settee, for the first time since he sat down on it. He went into the hall, closing the living room door behind him. When a man does this, whether automatically or by intent, the implication arises that he desires privacy. One cannot open the door again and stalk, or even tippy-toe, across the hall and into a kitchen bordering upon where he will be speaking. So Sally lingered in the living room. The dinner would come to no harm. Another miracle of modern technology.

When he had dialled, Tommy said softly, "Mario? Listen— there may be a copper in, asking questions. Pete Parsons, it could be. Get this: A couple of weeks or so ago—three herberts in, working a protection racket. Weekly payments, or they'd smash

31

us up. One tall, two short, all wearing jeans and studded leather-look jackets. You and Hans got rid of 'em. You don't have to go into details—all you know is, I called you over and you got rid of 'em. Tell Hans. All right?" He listened for a moment, while the phone spoke back in attractively accented English. Said, "Yes—yes—it's— She wouldn't have—they wouldn't have—the smoke would have—before the fire got to them. I'm—staying with friends. Be in tomorrow evening. Don't forget what I told you. Bye."

He hung up; stood for a moment with head bowed, the palms of his hands pressed against his eyes. Then he drew one deep, jagged sigh and went back to the living room. Sally could move out now.

Dinner passed the evening along a little. The cooker had done a good job, but Tommy ate almost nothing. Afterward they sat in front of the television, which had this one great virtue: You don't have to talk as you watch it. Dodging for Tommy's sake the channels featuring news programmes lumbered them with a wild-life repeat spying on the secret life and sexual peccadillos of an Outer Mongolian fruit bat of revolting aspect and a movie in the "All-Time Greats" series filmed through flickering rain before any of them was born, starring actors they had never heard of and didn't like now—Charlie and Sally didn't. God knows what Tommy was thinking about—as they emoted and shouted as if every throat were a rusty tin barrel. It was this or the video; and the video contained very funny films that would have gone down like the well-known lead balloon, tonight. At midnight they had one more drink, one more snack that Tommy did not touch. Then they went to bed.

Tommy showed his one flash of animation when Charlie went up with him to the guest room, acting the courteous host. He said with sudden vehemence, "I'll get the bastard, Charlie—I swear it. I'll get the bastard."

Startled—Tommy had swung round, eyes blazing in that sick white face—Charlie said, fatuously, "What bastard?"

"The sod who did it. I'll get him."

"Better leave that to old Pete," Charlie said. "If anybody can sort him—or them—out, it'll be Pete. Got everything you need? Good night then, mate." No good saying sleep well. Not with the things Tommy had on his mind.

Charlie went along to what was called in the chauvinist-pig house plans the Master Bedroom. Not far, it lay next door. Sally was there already, laying the last of her clothes neatly folded on the wicker chair at her side of the bed. She said,

"All right?"

"Yes, I suppose so. Says he's going to get the bastard who did it."

"How?" She turned to pick up her nightdress.

"Just talk. Good sign, really, if he's starting to show a bit of life." He was undoing his tie, feeling with one toe to kick off the other slipper. His second-best pair he was wearing, the others were set out in Tommy's room together with the spare pyjamas and the better dressing gown. "I said leave it to the police."

"Police." She spoke scathingly, lifting the flimsy gown to drop it over her head. Her shapely breasts rose and flattened slightly to the raising of her arms, the graceful curves of her body, the long, slim legs, the soft dark pubic hair very beautiful in the subdued lamplight.

"Don't underestimate the police. They have the facilities. They'll be using the rubber hoses on everybody known to have struck a match."

"You would say that." The nightgown dropped; semi-transparent, only half concealing. She picked up the bandana, to tie it over her hair. Dark hair cut short, with its own built-in bends. Not every woman is so lucky, and not every man. He never got clonked in the night with metal curlers stuck about like badger traps. She really was a very pretty girl. Not only that—she earned money. "Loyalty to the old firm. They never got old Harry's car back, did they?" She turned to the bed.

"This is different." He had his own masculine beauty, stepping

33

out of his slacks and standing naked while he shook them into their creases. They took care of their clothes, these two. Both were in professions that place value upon self-presentation. "They'll have every man in the area working on this one. And Pete won't let anything go by. Not with a mate concerned."

"Hard luck on anybody who's not a mate." She spoke from the bed, settling her head on the pillow.

"Turn it up." They were speaking quietly. The walls of these houses were pretty solid, but soft speaking is instinctive when the subject of the talking is right next door. "You know what I mean—Julie and the bab— Tommy—like part of the bloody family, isn't it? You'd get stuck into it yourself."

"Sorry," she said. "You're right." I don't know why I needle, she was thinking. It's been a horrible day, I guess I'm uptight. I *know* I'm uptight.

He was climbing into the pyjamas he seldom wore, joining her in the bed. They lay on their backs in silence for a while, before he said, "You'd have thought he'd have reported that protection lark, wouldn't you?"

"It's like he said, he didn't take it seriously. Hans and Mario are all he needs."

"That's not the point; if old Pete had pressed it he could have dropped in. Compounding an attempted felony. Something like that."

He turned towards her, moving so that one leg straddled hers as his hand went to her breast. She arrested the hand. "No," she said. "No—it's too hot."

"Too hot?" he said. "What's the flipping air conditioning for?" Actually, they nullified the air conditioning in here by sleeping with the windows open. But that was hardly the point. His hand was stilled. He never raped her. Never had need. But he moved his fingers slightly, caressing. Usually she responded quickly. Now she pushed him away firmly, said,

"No. Not with Tommy—it wouldn't feel right."

He knew what she meant. But he knew the tension in him,

built up over the awful day, and the matching tension in her; and this—this was the best way he knew to relieve tension. His body knew, too. He said,

"For God's sake—Tommy won't hear."

"The racket you make when you go over the top," she said, "I wonder you don't set the burglar alarm off."

"Hark who's talking," he said. "Tugboat Annie." But he took his hand away, drew off as she turned her back to him. When he spoke again it was after he had reached up to switch the light out, and he sounded sulky. "Don't blame me, then, if you can't sleep."

"Is that what we are now, then?" she said. "A couple of sleeping pills?"

It was two in the morning before they decided that this was silly, that Nature or Whoever designed it all knew best. Then they made love. And then they slept.

But Tommy did not sleep. He lay all night tortured by horror, gazing open-eyed into the darkness.

4

The following morning, Tommy went off to Chester. He said he was going as they sat at breakfast. Somebody had to break the news to his in-laws. Knowing police procedure, Charlie said, "They've probably been told already. Pete may have been on to the Chester police." He may not, of course. He hadn't asked Tommy how he wanted it handled.

"Doesn't make any difference, does it? I can't just ignore them." He looked sick still, and shattered; but some animation had come back to him.

"You could ring." As soon as Charlie said it he knew the suggestion did not stand up. A man cannot simply ring and say, "Hallo, Mum-in-law, your daughter is dead in a fire and so is your grandchild." Sure enough, Tommy vetoed it.

"No. I can't do that. I have to see them."

"Uh-huh," said Charlie. "I suppose you do. Will you be staying over?"

"I don't know. I'll have to—play it by ear. Depends on—how they take— I can do it and be back in a day. If that's all right."

Sally spoke. In deference to his presence here she was fully dressed. Usually, on the slack morning after her column-writing day, she breakfasted in her dressing gown. "Of course it is. Do you want anything to take with you? Sandwiches or—something?" A long drive, to Chester and back.

"No, Sal, thanks. I can get something on the road. I—appreciate it. Both of you. I appreciate—you know. Everything."

"Balls," said Charlie. A thing he seldom did with Sally there, when other people were present. In private he ripped it off now and again, quarrelling or at the time of hitting a thumb with the hammer. "Better leave us the phone number, in case we need to reach you. And we'd better let Pete know you're going." Poor old Tom—something may break. And they may fix the inquest for tomorrow—you'll be needed for that.

"Yes," said Tommy. "Yes. Right." He'd hardly touched his good eggs and bacon. But he had a scattering of cornflakes in him.

He went soon after, before Charlie left for the office. Another lovely morning, dew on the budding roses and the promise of great heat later. An ugly smell, though, from the desolation next door, and a jar to the eye that looked upon it.

Tommy did not. Charlie had moved his car into this drive, to have it off the road. He got in, wearing Charlie's shirt and underpants, and drove away without a sideways glance. Standing in the benevolent sunshine to watch him go—they both came out with him, quite unnecessarily; well, it showed their concern—Sally said,

"Poor old Tom. I hope he'll be all right."

"He forgot to ring Pete," said Charlie. "And I forgot to remind him."

"Doubt if Pete's in yet."

"Bet he is. He won't be working half past nine to five on this job. If he's not, I'll get him at home."

He was in. When he was told that Tommy had gone to Chester, he said, "Yeah. That's all right, so long as we can get hold of him. Not going to be a very happy trip for him. I was going to ring later, to see if he wanted us to break it to them, he was in no state to bother with it yesterday."

"You been up all night?"

"No. No, I got a few hours in the sack. Didn't sleep much, though, this lark was on my mind. I've been working on our known bugs, I think we can count 'em all out. And I'll tell you something that surprises me a bit: We don't know of any protec-

37

tion mob operating. None of the other restaurants or bookies or anybody in the area's been approached. I went in to see Mario and Hans last night, they don't know much. Tommy called 'em over and they saw the geezers off."

"Well—like Tom said—little herberts, trying it on for size. Took one look at Hans and said, 'Sod this, it's back to mugging old ladies.'"

"Yes. I'd like a word with 'em, though; if they're regular clients I'd like 'em to know the beady's on them. But Mario and Hans didn't notice much more about them than Tommy did."

"You don't reckon they put the petrol in?"

"Never know, do you? You don't know, these days. The whole bloody caper's gone mad, they burn up Pakistanis for the kicks. Ah well—we'll plug away at it. Tell you something—I was looking at Suzie last night. Thinking—you know. Doesn't bear thinking about, does it?"

Suzie was Mrs. Parsons. Growing plump, but still comely. Charlie had fancied her too, more than once in his boisterous fantasies. "I know what you mean," he said.

Pete was speaking again. "I'll get the bastards, Charlie, I swear it. I'll get the bastards."

"Precisely what Tommy said." Precisely, word for word. Only he used the singular.

"Don't let him start piddling about," said Pete. "It's no game for amateurs. I'll ring about the inquest, sure to be tomorrow. See you, son." He hung up the phone and was gone.

Charlie went into the kitchen, where Sally was putting the breakfast things in the washing-up machine. With Pete's words fresh in his mind he looked at her. She was very lovely—not merely as Sally, but as a beautiful example of a beautiful species. And she, he knew by her fretting if she got a pimple, her fussiness over makeup and dress when they went out, had very little confidence in her own beauty. Women, he had come to realize by observing outward from his experience of her, never do have. It accounts for their bitchiness, their unrestrainable jealousies. It

38

accounts for Marilyn Monroe and all the lovely women whose lack of confidence kills, and makes quack beauticians and charlatan psychiatrists wealthy.

Unaware of his watching until she rose from the machine-loading and turned to face him, every line of her, every movement offered grace, entirely without deliberate intent. Long ago she had discarded bras, except when for some evening function she decided against the evidence that the whole thing needed bracing up a bit; so now there was tiny movement under the blouse and a hint of nipples when the thin material clung. Finding his eyes upon her, she said, "What are you looking at?" A touch of suspicion even in this, as though he had become transfixed by a sudden wart.

He felt pure love for her sweep over him. Not for a long time had he felt it: the touch of awe that he had access, by right of mutual need, to a creature so beautiful; the inner weeping sympathy for her humanity, her fears, her smallness. He said, "You. You're lovely." And it could have been you, all destroyed. Julie was as lovely as you are, and as live.

"Ah," she said. "Mm." She stood there looking back at him, uncertainly.

He moved, and took her into his arms. Held her close, one hand stroking her hair, her arms holding him. When he moved his hand now to her breast she made no objection. At last she raised her head and her eyes looked into his. "Isn't it a pity?" she said. "The quarrelling lately? Why do we do it?"

"I don't know," said Charlie. "I suppose we're just bloody stupid."

"Speak for yourself," she said. But no umbrage in it. Just lovers' predictable silliness.

"I love you," he told her. "You know that, don't you?"

She smiled. "No time to do anything about it now. Let go. Get out of here and fetch me back some money."

It was just like old times.

39

Tommy did not come home that night. Nor did he ring. They sat up late waiting for him, wondering if they should try the Chester number he had given them. Decided against it, neither one desiring to blurt in on what could have been a family crisis, collapse perhaps of parents whose world had disintegrated with the news that daughter and grandchild were dead. But, as Sally said, "You'd have thought he'd ring, wouldn't you? He said he would." To tell them whether or not he would be back tonight.

"We don't know what happened when he got there. Or he may have broken down or something, on the way home."

"There are phone booths. He could have reversed the charges, if he hadn't got any change."

"Mm. Well—we might as well go to bed. He'll turn up. Poor old lad—I don't envy him the inquest." It was set for tomorrow, after he had confirmed identity. Pete rang, to say so. Today, if you reckon from now—it was two o'clock, and yet another lovely night.

"Don't envy any of us," Sally said. They had decided that one of them, if not both, must attend with him, to render moral support.

He was not back when they got up in the morning, and the telephone still had not rung. They breakfasted alone in a silence that threw into high relief the very chomping of cereals. Sally had an assignment this morning, and Charlie was due at the office as usual. They pinned a note to the front door when they stepped out into the sunshine, and Charlie said before they drove away in their separate cars,

"Bye then, love. If he hasn't rung me by lunchtime I'll give old Pete a buzz. Not that there's anything to worry about."

In the event it was Pete who rang him, at about the time when sensible workers break up the morning with coffee and biscuits. He said, "I've been trying your house, thought Tommy might be there. Got no answer. How is he?"

"He hasn't come back," Charlie told him.

"Oh." A pause. "Did he ring or anything?"

"Nope. Not a word."

"Ah. I was hoping he might be able to give me a bit more about the protection herberts. Or he might have thought of something else." He did not have to add, "People often do, when receding shock allows resumption of direct thinking." Charlie as a one-time policeman would know that. "He hasn't said any more to you?"

"We haven't seen him since yesterday morning."

"Mm. I'm a bit stuck, can't get on to any protection racket being worked—nothing. All right, mate—when he turns up, tell him I'd like a word. Keep your hand on your halfpenny."

Charlie put the phone down. From that well-tarted inner office came the high fluting of fat Bert Porter. "That Pete Parsons?" A fair assumption, Charlie had said "Hi, Pete," right at the start of the call.

"Yep."

Fat Bert had heard his every word, and an insurance investigator needs no more than half a telephone conversation. He said, "I know this geezer's your mate, but he wouldn't have scarpered, would he?"

"Why the bloody hell should he scarper?" Charlie snapped.

"How the bloody hell would I know? I'm not the Old Bill, I'm just a geezer with terrible piles trying to turn an honest crust."

You're just an obese slob, grown paranoic from too long trying to fiddle out of any claim that so much as sniffs a little wonky, Charlie snarled in silence, but his own experience was whispering, deep in his mind: Could it be? The rest of him was saying, Don't be bloody stupid.

It was after lunch when Pete rang again. "Charlie? Pete. Any sign of Tommy?"

"Nope. Nothing."

41

"That's what I thought, been trying the house again. I've been on to the parents at Chester. He never arrived."

"What?" said Charlie.

"Had to break the news—fell right into it, didn't I? Wasn't pleasant, they reckon they're coming down. He didn't ring them, he didn't arrive. They haven't seen him since Christmas."

"Amnesia?" Charlie said. "Wandered off? Shock? Delayed effect?"

"Could be," said Pete. "I reckon it's very likely. I've got an EMTAD out, we ought to gather him up soon." An EMTAD is shorthand speech for Express Message to All Districts. It goes out to every force within a specified area, or throughout the country. "There's another thing. I've been digging about. Tommy is Julie's second husband. Did you know that?"

"No." Surprise, surprise.

"Well, he is. Was. He was co-respondent, and the other geezer's a nutter. Went right off his rocker over it. They put him inside, he's been swearing ever since that he'd do 'em."

"Where is he now, this nutter?"

"They let him out, couple of weeks ago. He's vanished, too."

"Christ," said Charlie.

"Yeah, I know. They say he's recovered, but he's supposed to be checking in and he hasn't. I've put a call out for him, too."

"You don't think he's—grabbed old Tom, do you?" Bombed the house—found Tommy wasn't in it—lurked about, unseen and unsuspected. Grabbed him before he knew what was on. Easy enough—follow his car. Somewhere, he has to stop. Draw in behind—slip in beside him. With a gun? Kill him? Christ.

"Charlie mate—you know and I know, anything's possible. I could be going off half-cock, he could turn up any minute. I'm sorting out the possibilities, that's all."

It's all you can do, Charlie thought, at the moment. You'll have the route to Chester covered, now you have to wait. "Uh-huh," he said. "Well—we just have to wait."

"Yep. I'll get back to you, if anything comes up. Is Fatso there?"

"Yes, he's in his office."

"Tell him to get stuffed."

When the phone went down, the peculiar voice fluted again. "Pete?"

"Yes," said Charlie. "Said to tell you to get stuffed."

"I should be so lucky," the fat man said. There was rue in it.

When Charlie got home in the evening, Sally was out. She rang him at the office late in the afternoon to say she would be. A demonstration of Javanese cookery in the town, given by a cooking lady well known on television and marked as meat course for the next column. Normally Sally would have worked from copy supplied by Nicky Carter, attending on her behalf; she herself having chatted for the human-interest angle with the lady by day, in her hotel. But Nicky broke an ankle falling down the town-hall steps, having gone there to beard the mayor about a bus shelter, so Sally must do it herself.

This was the thing Charlie hated, this coming home to an empty house, eating on the way, or going out later to eat, or rooting around in the fridge and tinned-food cupboard to fix something for himself. It happened often—necessarily, a good deal of her material was gathered during the evenings, at meetings and the like. Nicky could not cover them all, she was regular reporting staff and Harry wouldn't have allowed it. So the empty-house routine came to Charlie often. Too bloody often, in his opinion.

It was one of the chief bones of increasing contention between them. Chauvinism in the male, secret guilt lingering in the working female are by no means dead, especially when the wife, at odds with a primary feminine raison d'être, is pitted against children, and her mate is only half developed, kept short of maturity by lack of responsibility for his own vulnerable seedlings.

He sniped at her work, snide malice nowadays laid over what

43

used to be loving teasing. She snapped back, more and more spitefully—in resentment, and because centuries of social custom nags in woman, and she cannot slough off that guilt. He was glad enough of the money, she said, when he was switching from police to insurance and making humpence a week. Even now, she said, they couldn't live the way they did if she didn't work.

All true enough. Charlie still hated coming home to an empty house. A fine house, yes, the feet did not echo on bare lino. But the very carpet imposed indifferent silence, wall to bloody wall.

Tonight he was not liking it, but there was no resentment in him. This morning's surge of feeling for her had swept away the late year's tarnishing trivia. He missed her. Well, he always did, it was the basis of his irritability. But tonight he missed her not for his purely chauvinist sake, but for her loved and vulnerable, one-day-to-be-old sake. And missing her, he desired her even as he heated up a tin of soup and defrosted a bone-hard steak in the microwave oven. His mind twitching between her and the Tommy situation, he flexed to ease the pressure and thought, There's another thing you ought to be grateful for—we've got this jolly sex-life. Without it, we'd probably have squabbled our way into the divorce court. I think we're over-sexed, thank God.

Tommy had not turned up. Not here, at any rate. And Pete had not rung again, so presumably he'd heard nothing. Eating his soup straight out of the pretty saucepan, clapping the steak between two slices of bread because he could not be bothered to fiddle with vegetables, he thought about ringing Pete and decided against it. The lad would be busy, and he'd expect an ex-pro to know that no phone call meant he had nothing to pass along.

Munching his fat sandwich, he switched on and sat in front of the television, on the settee where Tommy had spent all of yesterday. Bloody rubbish. It was always bloody rubbish when he was alone here in the evening, no matter how he clicked from channel to channel. He could put a cassette on, see a feature film over again. But truth to tell, he was sick of telly and all its shiny adjuncts. He could put the hi-fi on; but he didn't feel like music.

44

Didn't even like it all that much; Sally was the one who dug the Beethoven.

He'd go out. Into the country, it was a lovely evening. He'd drive out Seton Magnum way, sit on the bench outside the Red Lion with a pint. It was rarely enough one had the weather for it. Make the most of this lot. There might be evening cricket to watch; if a team was a man short he might pick up a game. Grey slacks were all right, for a substitute, and he'd put on a white shirt.

A quick shower, a change of shirt, and he went out to his car. Nobody about next door, but somebody had been there during the day. Fixed to the front gate was a notice: DANGER. KEEP OUT. Driving away, he considered calling at the house opposite to see how old Fellows was doing. But Mrs. Fellows would keep him nattering, picking her relishing way through the bones of it. He couldn't stand the woman, her teeth kept slipping. He drove on.

At the end of the street, about to turn right, he thought: No. I'll go and see Mario. It's not barging in on police business—you never know, he may remember something he forgot to tell Pete. Or I may think of something Pete didn't think to ask. I don't really feel like swanning about. Not with things as they are.

So he turned left. Right for the country, Seton Magnum and beyond; left to the town centre.

The Belle Epoque stood in a quaint byway, just off the central shopping precinct. Tommy bought it little more than a year ago, a going concern but in a sadly run-down condition. Julie guided him in the refurbishing of it, and she had flair. They'd knocked down a wall, but she said keep the low ceilings, it's nice and intimate. Touch the beams up, people like beams. Make the most of them. So he did.

Inside now the ambiance was cosy, and rosy with concealed lighting augmenting the coloured candles that decorated with multi-tinted waxes the bottles in which they were set. Easily done: When you fish out a stub you insert a candle differently coloured. Outside, the beams were matte-blackened—not many

Tudor buildings left in the town, but this was one of them—the stucco between a shining white. Very popular it proved, right from the opening party.

Most of the cricket club brought their wives here, high days and anniversaries, because it didn't come cheap. Tommy unobtrusively knocked a bit off for them, and always coughed up a bottle of his very special wine with his compliments; but even so . . . Charlie and Sally, both earning good money, came quite often. Would have come more, but didn't like to because of the free wine. And a rose for the lady from a Neapolitan head man is lovely, now and again; but both you and he get a bit embarrassed if, having instituted the custom, he has to do it twice a week. These beaming little niceties can backfire.

Nobody known to Charlie was in tonight. Not many people here at all. When recession dips into depression, no high-price restaurant can expect to fill all the time. Perhaps, too, the vogue was passing. A new and amusing roadhouse had opened out on the bypass. It was called the Dolloping Duckling, and that alone is definitely amusing. We'll meet at the Dolloping Duckling, darling. Isn't it a *scream?*

Mario was hovering at a table, using his devastating, wavy-haired, slimly elegant charm on a grey-haired, simpering lady with a bald but tolerant husband, while brick-built Hans, showing astonishing delicacy, landed little potatoes and twigs of broccoli, every one on the plate. Mario himself poured a little of his recommended wine, for the ritual tasting. Time tonight for the full treatment. A natural head waiter, Mario, a very good manager, and he ran a tight ship. When he saw Charlie he made his divine little bow to the lady and left her fluttering. "Ah—Meestair Wood," he purred as he approached, white teeth spread for inspection like something dreamed up and proudly honed for a toothpaste ad. "And where is *la bella signora* theese eevening?" They were actually capped. In Liverpool, of all places.

"I'm not staying, Mario," Charlie said. "Can I have a word with you?"

Mario asked no questions. He would have known, of course, the entire situation regarding Tommy. His beam moderated. "Let us go into the keetchen, Meestair Wood," he said. Rightly, and very obviously, as a good pro he did not want his innocent feeders listening in. They would know nothing of the troubles, nothing of the connection between restaurant owner and fire. They probably would not overhear; but it is unprofessional for the presiding genius to stand whispering with a big man not wearing a jacket, who leaves afterwards without stopping to eat. People paying £7 for a grilled sole—admittedly, with a subtle sauce—expect while they eat it to be insulated from all things indecorous and smacking of the sinister. They want to be in Fairyland. Many fairies, indeed, make a vocation out of pandering to the wish.

As they turned toward the baize-fronted door leading to the kitchen, the curtain covering the street entrance opened and Pete Parsons appeared, jacket draped over one arm and his tie pulled awry. He looked hot and weary, and the eye with which he fixed Charlie had something of suspicion in it. "Thought you'd be in here," he said. "Saw your car. Time for a word, Mario?"

"Een the keetchen, Meestair Pete," said Mario. He led the way. Hans watched them go from under his brows as he stood with massive head bent, spooning that subtle sauce onto the bald man's plate. "That'll do, Hans," the bald man said good-humouredly. "Don't want it all floating about, do we?"

The kitchen was spotless, rich with the hot odours of good food. Two men in clean aprons and tall white hats worked here—a chef and a commis chef, both French. Mario ignored them. He said, "What can I do for you, Meestair Pete?"

Five minutes later he ushered them out again, having answered Pete's questions readily—the policeman having arrived, Charlie asked none—without adding any remembered detail to what he said before. The three tearaways were just tearaways, jeans and leather jackets, one tall, two short. No, he did not know of any enemies, everybody liked Meestair Tommee and Signora Julie. And the *bambino*—terrible. Terrible. No, he had not

seen Meestair Tommee since the fire. Just one telephone call—
last night—to say he would not be in. No—he had no idea where
Meestair Tommee could be. Chestair? No, Meestair Tommee
had not told him he was going to Chestair. But then, why should
he? He, Mario, often went for days, weeks, without seeing Meestair Tommee or knowing where he was.

"All right, Mario. Thanks," Pete said at last. He'd expected no
more; he'd hoped, as Charlie did, that some tiny fact might come
to him from the Italian sufficient to give him some sort of lead.
All day, he and many others, higher up and lower, had worked on
the case, and found none.

"My pleasure, Meestair Pete," Mario said. From habit, surely?
There was not much pleasure about. "Anyteeng I can do, plizz
let me know. Anyteeng."

"I'll do that," Pete assured him, and they followed him back
into the restaurant where they bade him goodbye and left. When
they were gone Mario began to check the items on a customer's
bill. Hans, detouring to pass close on the way with empty dishes
to the kitchen, murmured, "Vot dey vant?"

"Not now, not now," said Mario, softly and savagely. "Not
now, for Christ's sake." Noticeably less accent than he used for
his public persona. And they had to communicate in English: He
had no German, and Hans no Italian.

Outside in the street, Pete Parsons said, "Where do you go
from here?"

"Nowhere, really," Charlie told him. "Sally's out, some bloody
cookery caper. I'm just killing time."

"Pint?"

"Don't see why not."

They went to the Green Man, which was just along the road in
another good old building. Reprehensibly tarted, but with the
beamed main fabric still more or less intact. People will go without food sooner than forswear liquor, so recession bites less pain-

fully into brewers than into restaurateurs. There was a fair crowd here. Seated at the bar with pint in hand, Pete said,

"I hope you're not playing Lord Peter Wimsey."

"Killing time, that's all. Thought Mario might have remembered something I could pass on to you."

"Don't overdo it, mate. All we want is bloody amateurs blundering about."

Charlie might have pointed out that he'd been for ten years professional. And insurance investigating is not characterized by blundering about. But Pete was tired and edgy, he'd had a hard, frustrating day. Charlie knew those days very well. So he answered mildly, "Don't worry. What about Tommy?"

"Nothing." The chunky policeman brooded into his beer. Not often he scowled, he had one of those faces shaped to light up with chuckle and beam. "Not a bloody thing. Not even his car. Nothing. Can't even come up with the protection outfit. And all our firebugs are alibied."

"It'll come," said Charlie. Cases often do begin with hiatus. It screws the nerves of policemen. Pete would be more than normally screwed, because of the personal element. He was speaking again.

"The guv'nor has theories."

The guv'nor on this job, Charlie remembered, under the Chief Constable, was Detective Chief Superintendent Billy the Fumer Fumery. He'd have to form theories to cope with his own frustrated fuming. "What are they?"

Pete swigged at his pint before putting it down so that he could use his fingers to enumerate. "One—amnesia. Shock. Wandered off."

"I go with that."

"Two—second favourite—he blew out a bunch of herberts setting up a protection racket and they bombed him for persuasion and publicity, to scare the shit out of other clients. Only we haven't found any other clients."

"Maybe they scared the shit out of themselves, when they knew about Julie and the nipper. Maybe they slung it in."

"Could be. Could be. Three: that Julie's nutcase ex-husband did it, and now he's grabbed Tom. They can be bloody scary, these nutters, they do things before you even know they're there. And we haven't turned him up, either."

"I didn't even know Julie was married before. They never mentioned it."

"Nor did I, but we've found things out. He used to belt her—he's a paranoid schizophrenic. She was old Tom's secretary."

"Where was all this?"

"In the city, before they moved here. It's all in the files, our lads were called and the bloke went into the hutch. Tom had taken her away. The geezer did his nut, Parry his name is, Clifton Parry. Found out where they were living, tried to force his way in. Attacked old Tom, but I don't know who won. She got a divorce. No—he did. Cited Tom."

"Nice. Very nice."

"Uh-huh. Now they've let him out again. And we can't find him. Marvellous, isn't it? And he swore he'd do 'em both."

Silence for a moment. He swigged morosely. Charlie said, "Any more?"

"Four," said Pete, ticking off another finger, "Tommy knows who did it, or thinks he does. And he's gone off looking for him."

"Or them? The tearaways?"

"Tom may have invented them, he says, to keep us happy while he gets on with it. Cobblers to that, *I* say. It implicates Mario and Hans.

"Five: Tommy knows who did it and he's run for cover, shit-scared. Which means something bent's going on and Tom's connected with it. It also means the bugs are bigger than our three little herberts. But Hans and Mario confirm the herberts. Who might have been working for the big boys.

"Six: Tommy may know who did it, counting out the nutter—didn't mention him to us, did he, old Tom?—or he may not; but whoever it is wanted him, found he'd missed him, and hung about until he or they could grab him."

A further short silence. Charlie broke it. "Done a bit of theorizing, our Billy, hasn't he?"

"Huh." A disparaging noise.

"What do you think?"

"I think Billy gets on my tits. I think it's amnesia, or the nutter—either he's grabbed Tom, or Tom knew it was him and he's gone to get him. That'd be why he didn't mention him to us, he wanted him all to himself. And he can land himself right in the steaming."

"You can't blame him, though, can you? I mean, you couldn't if he did."

"I'm not blaming him, I'm worrying about him, that's all. Sod it—I can't officially even treat him as a missing person. Nobody's reported him."

"I reported him."

"You don't count. You didn't ring me, I rang you. And he's only been gone a day or so. Tell you another thing—keep all this under your hat, I don't know why I'm telling you, they'd have my guts—we haven't been able to find out where Tom was the night of the fire."

"Didn't ask him, did you?" That would have been easy enough.

"Didn't even think of it. Didn't matter, did it? But Billy started filling in time, poking into everything, and nobody's come up to tell us where he was."

"Who's he asked, for Christ's sake?"

"Don't ask me, I'm just the hired help. Somebody'll come forward, is my belief, when we've stuck his clock in the papers."

"Are you putting him in the papers, then?"

"Big and beaming. HAVE YOU SEEN THIS MAN? Blow-up from last year's team photo, it's the only one I had. Well—if you're buying another beer, I'll stick around. If you're not, I'm buggering off."

"I bought this one."

"That's what I thought you'd say. So I'm buggering off. I'll buy us another, though, before I go." The humour was back in the policeman's eye. It had always done him good, a natter with Charlie. He called for two more pints.

At about this time, the man came to Tommy in the cellar where he sat on an old flock mattress, all trussed up with his back against the wall. There was a bump on his head from when he had been hit suddenly with the butt of a gun as he walked from his car, stopped in a layby, to a nearby phone booth from which he had been intending to ring Mario, with necessary instructions, and a pounding agony in his skull; because only in lurid books and bad movies can a man be hit like that and come up next minute all fighting fit. He felt dreadful, and he was scared. Very scared.

The man came into the cellar from the one door, preceded by a grating of bolts, an audible turning of key. That sound of the key turning against stiffness suggested that the cellar was not in regular use. It made no difference, so far as Tommy was concerned. He was not evaluating his surroundings, looking for factors to aid escape as the heroes do. He was plain, honest-to-Jesus scared.

The man came down the stairs, making no clack on the bare stone. So he must have changed into slippers, because he'd clacked when he went up. Tommy was not noticing this, either. He was looking up at the man, who seemed to be staring down at him from a great height, saying, "Ah. You're looking better. That's good, I thought perhaps you'd been hit too hard. It's easily done, you know; the skull is more vulnerable than people believe. That's why boxing is so dangerous. Cumulative brain damage."

He paused, almost as though inviting conversational rejoinder. None came, of course. No chance of it, through the thick Elastoplast stuck across Tommy's mouth. After a moment he carried on.

"You should never have done it, you know. You should have known better. Where has it got you in the end? You're going to die, that's where it's got you. All your nice home burned down and everything. All because you couldn't keep your hands off other people's property."

He paused again. Tommy's eyes looked up at him, beseeching. Through the gagging stretch-bandage came a muffled, desperate grunting.

"The only question is," the man said, "how to do it? Mm? One quick shot—perhaps there—right between the eyes." He pointed a finger, directing it like a gun. "Or something a little more painful, to enhance the personal pleasure? To me, of course. Not to you." And he laughed.

He watched for a moment Tommy's grunting panic, his wriggling on the flock mattress as he struggled with the bonds that held him. Then he said, "It's really no good, they're all sticky tape. No knots in them to be undone like they do in the pictures. No handy bits of metal about, to cut through them. James Bond might manage it. But you're not James Bond, are you? You're Thomas Neil Grover, known to his friends as Tommy. But I call you scum, because I'm not one of your friends. Am I?"

Now he moved away. At the top of the stairs he turned to say: "The question of food. I don't suppose it interests you at the moment, I doubt if you are hungry. But it will in time, if I don't kill you first. It's just occurred to me that it might be fun to simply keep you here, let you starve to death. Or die from thirst—I believe that's *very* unpleasant." He opened the door; spoke again. "I shall turn the light off. You don't have to worry about rats, I don't believe we have any. But of course, I could be wrong."

The light switch clicked, the yellow rectangle left vanished as the door closed. The key turned, the bolts grabbed. The man was gone.

5

All that was on Friday. On Saturday morning nothing seemed to be happening. Things were, of course; but they moved beneath the surface. Many policemen were working, Hans was approaching a condition of sweating fear—but from where Sally and Charlie stood, nothing appeared to be stirring. Tommy was pictured in the papers, grinning in his cricket whites, a blown-up portion of the same group photo that Charlie had in a drawer. His disappearance was mentioned on the BBC radio news. That happened publicly, and nothing more.

Charlie was not deceived. He knew what work must be going on, in and out of the police station. But Sally fretted. She said,

"You'd think Pete would at least ring. He must know we're worried."

"He'll be up to the rump. No reason why he should ring us."

"No reason? He's a friend, isn't he? And we're all Tommy's friends. And Tommy vanished from here. And you were Pete's oppo all those years, you're practically a copper even now."

"I'm a civilian. You're a civilian. Nobody's got to tell us anything."

"We're friends—"

"Coppers don't go around spilling everything to their friends. Not to their civvy friends. There's an official-secrets act, they can get done if they do."

"What's official secret about Tommy? He's not a Russian spy, is he?"

"Oh, come on, Sal, you're not that bloody dumb. I'm surprised old Pete's said as much as he has." And flattered, rather. He's trusted me, as friend of Tom and of him. He's trusted me as brother copper.

"Sorry," Sally said. "Bit edgy. Take no notice. And don't call me Sal."

"Old Pete'll ring when he's got something to tell us. He knows how we're feeling.

At lunchtime, Tommy's Belle Epoque opened as usual. No reason for it not to, simply because the boss had vanished; Mario was not the man to miss the Saturday trade. Besides stray tourists wandering the quainter section of the town and attracted by the beamed and gabled, beautifully clean façade, there was a solid nucleus of local couples who lunched there as a treat to lighten the chore of Saturday shopping. Several businessmen, too, shop owners and the like, came in every day of the week.

So today, Mario presided as usual. Immaculate, urbane as ever, smiling his brilliant smile, charming with his accent; quipping where a quip was right and proper, bending solicitously over middle-aged lady customers—never over young ones, the escort might object—to guide to a right choice from the menu. Right from his point of view, his suggestions controlled by what was hanging fire in the kitchen. Beckoning to Hans—meticulously totalling bills before their presentation—smiling—smiling—smiling—if he was worried, it did not show.

With big Hans, it was rather different. He worked well enough, with no falling away in his strange, almost feminine deftness; but he did it all in silence, worry showing in the increased heaviness of his set face.

None of the customers noticed. He never did sparkle, that was Mario's province. Bewitched by Mario, they liked Hans for his deftness, they remarked upon his size, the regulars greeted him by name; but he was not expected to whistle while he worked. If secret lust for him brought some of the women back, even they did not dream about his happy-go-lucky personality. Today, certainly, happy-go-luckiness was more than usually far away.

Mario knew what ailed him, and beneath the smooth exterior it bothered him. The big man was unpredictable under stress, even his boxing career proved it. He'd have been world class, but for an ineradicable penchant for going wild under pressure, of doing the wrong thing. It got him knocked out. Too often. Not that he was punchy, or anything like it; but he was a man who, looking rugged and rocklike, could turn out to be the link that snapped.

Mario was playing for his whole life. For renewed honour among his confreres, for a future where he would no longer fawn and scrape, except to certain men of great power. With their favour, with monies due and to come, he might open a restaurant of his own—a chain of restaurants; superb restaurants, not in this pig-swill country—in Paris—Roma—Napoli—all over. But he might not do that—he might be able simply to lie on warm beaches, drive only the best and most beautiful cars, ride only the best and most beautiful women.

Now he worried, deep down: about Hans, about the vanishing of Tommy, about the men who could have done it—fire-bombed Tommy and spirited him away, finding they had missed him there.

The implications were terrifying. If they did that to Tommy Grover—

And Hans—if Hans cracked and ran to the police—

The big man came swinging wide to pass within muttering distance, on his way through to the kitchen. He was doing too much of that, today. His fear seemed to demand close contact. Mario stood in his favoured position fronting the small wine dispensary and watched him come, the smile touching his lips still but gone from his eyes. Hans muttered,

"Ve cannot touch it tonight. Must be left dere."

"Shut up," Mario hissed. "Get on with your work, we'll discuss it when we close." He widened his smile, moved forward to greet new arrivals. "Ah—good day, signora—good day, sair. So naice—you have not been weeth us for long time. Table for two? Cairtainly. You are well? Happy? Good—good." The customers were beaming as he showed them to their table.

It is not often, in England where the strange rite originated, that cricket can be played in glorious sunshine with sweat glands working furiously under the white flannels. It was designed for this kind of weather, and the memories of old cricketers dwell upon the occasions, usually long ago, when sun and cricket fused to create perfection in living; but normally the playing time is spent peering morosely out from the pavilion at a rain-lashed field, or shivering under layers of white sweaters with blue fingers clutching at a venomously slippery ball.

But when June heat-wave and cricket do come together—ah. Then one sees what the ancients, cobbling together in their wisdom a red sphere, whittling a branch to whack it with, dreamed that it would be like. They knew, perhaps, how unlikely it was that they would ever live themselves to see it, but clinging to the dream nonetheless, they pressed on, as a man will plant an avenue of trees for the delight of future generations.

Today they were justified, blessed be their graves. A foretaste of Paradise, for the visiting team, and not even spoiled entirely— because the glory of cricket is in the game itself, rather than in the result—for the home team led by Tony Scully, who were in for a shellacking.

They were unsettled, that was the trouble. They all liked Tommy, they all teased and petted toddling Mandy, as they teased and petted all attached children, partly from social obligation, partly because it was nice to have them around. They all, except for a couple who were secretly gay, enjoyed Julie—her legs, her good body, her social charm when she took her turn doing the teas with other wives; who also were shocked and grieving, and shaken.

She should have been there in the pavilion today, laying out the lettuce and tinned meat, measuring tea into the big pot. Sally's being there instead, paired with Tony Scully's lady, only served to keep fresh in the minds of players and wives alike the reason why Julie and the bab were not. And Tommy gone missing.

Tommy was missed as a player, too; he opened the batting and could be relied upon so far as any ball game's unpredictability allows, to make runs. As could Pete Parsons, stylish at number four and able to hit, when set, like nobody since Arnold Tuckett, blacksmith, who cleared the very elms and smashed the church clock in 1864. The elms have gone, Dutch disease; but the dent is there still in the rim of the clock. What's more, they'd need Pete's fiery bowling when the jubilant opposition buckled on its pads and abdominal protector and marched cockahoop to the wicket. But Pete was working.

Charlie was doing pretty well. Opened the batting with a new young partner who went for nothing and started the rout. Stayed while the wickets crashed around him, most of the runs made were credited to him. They were not many. He was still there when yet another partner left for the pavilion and Tony Scully emerged, giraffe-tall and gangling in his pads and whites, batting well down the order because he was a good captain, deadly bowler at times, but no great shakes with the bat. When he was close he signalled Charlie for a mid-wicket conference, and all he could say, with gloom, was:

"Don't go for the runs, we'll just try to stay. We don't want to take 'em in for tea yet."

Negative, but understandable. Given a two-thirty start, tea should be taken after four o'clock. Maybe four-thirty, depending upon how long the first team bats. Divides the game nicely, with the second team's innings to come. Embarrassing, to be all out by three-fifteen and the water not even boiling yet in the urn. That leads to fuming and the curled lip among presiding wives. And what if the whole bloody match is over an hour before the pub opens? Now there is a nasty thought.

So Charlie said, "Right," and turned away; and was out the very next ball. Played forward, the bloody thing twisted and he heard the off-stump click as the fielder led by the happy, happy bowler hollered their awful cry, "Za-a-aat?" and went up in the air, the bowler highest of them all. No need to wait for the umpire's lifted finger, if he bothered to lift it. Charlie was on his way.

He went from the bright, grass-scented sunshine into the cooler pavilion, lifting his bat on the way to acknowledge a scatter of applause from team mates and the few spectators basking on wooden benches bordering the field. "Hard luck, Charlie," said his mates, none of whom had done so well; and "Nice innings, Charlie boy." "Ta," he said, making his way to the changing room, to get rid of pads and gloves and metal genital cup. When he emerged, Sally popped out from the kitchen to say crossly:

"You might have hung on a bit longer, we haven't even got the sandwiches done."

"That's cricket," he said. No point in snapping that you didn't miss the bloody thing on purpose, the edginess was simmering in her.

"Cricket," she snapped. "Bah!" And she popped back again. Didn't really like cricket, few of the wives did. It was just something you had to put up with, if you married a cricketing man. And the social side brought compensation. Even doing the teas was fun. Had been. Until this week.

He walked in his studded boots out from the shadowed pavilion onto the fretwork balcony, all the green-and-gold world spread before him, good country behind and the foreground mobile with the players' white figures. In a corner of the balcony distanced from where the home team sat on the benches in a group quieter than usual, because of Tommy and their own abject failure, stood Pete Parsons, and Pete was looking at him.

Charlie crossed. He said, "Hi, Pete. Didn't expect to see you." And, nodding to the shamed scoreboard on the far side of the ground: "Bloody shambles, annit? Better get your whites on."

"Don't know how you managed it," said Pete. "Soon as I turn my back." But this, clearly, was not what he had on his mind.

Charlie spoke more softly. "Anything?"

"Not a stiver." Pete's answer was as soft, or softer. "Nothing. Vanished."

"Bastard," said Charlie.

They stood for a moment, only their eyes looking outward over the field. The last man in, eyes averted, edged a single. "COME ON!!" bellowed Tony Scully, flapping full-tilt down the pitch in a tangle of arms and legs and pads like a lunatic ostrich as the lad stood bemused, wondering where that one went. Seeing Tony looming, assailed by the shout, he started violently and ran like the clappers for the other end. "Cricketers?" said Pete. "I've shot 'em. Did you know he had form?"

"Who had form?"

"Tommy."

"What? You're kidding."

"Wish I bloody was. Seven years ago, in Gloucester."

"Who says so?"

"The Gloucester police. We sent his prints round with the picture. Wasn't difficult, he borrowed my bat last week."

"What made you do that?" Tommy wasn't suspected of anything. Routine, to send out dabs of a suspected person, but not of the innocent.

Pete's voice took on a touch of almost defensive hardness. Obviously, he was not enjoying this. "We're not talking about stolen bicycles. When it turns this nasty we need every bit of background we can get, on *everybody*. You know that. Tom did time. Drew five, served three."

"*Five?* What did he do?" You don't draw five for a peccadillo.

"Burned down his cinema."

"*What?*" One or two of the team glanced over. Charlie's voice had risen. Pete waited, until they were back with the cricket.

"He owned this big cinema. Losing money. Went for the insurance. Got a pro in to do the job, geezer called Melvyn Kelly.

When the police got on to Tom he grassed, we've got all the records. Lumbered this Kelly, and the Gloucester lads only needed that, they'd had him before and there was a lot of stuff they knew was him and couldn't pin it. Well, they made enough of it stick and on top of Tom's lot it got him ten."

"Ten?" That's very thick porridge.

"Manslaughter came into it; a watchman died in one of his other capers. Specialist in setting fires. London—Manchester— you name it, I was talking to the Gloucester lads. Ten. With remission. You work it out."

"Bloody hell," Charlie said.

"Exactly. We've checked, and he's out. So now we've got another nutter loose, swearing he's going to get Tom. Swore it when he went in, anyway."

"Have you had him picked up?"

"Be your age. We've added him to the wanteds. Not a hope. Like I said, he's loose somewhere. No visits to the after-care people, nothing. We may turn him up easy—we haven't known about him all that long—or we may not. Puts a different look on old Tom, though, doesn't it?"

"Ah. Mm." It did that.

For a moment they were silent. End of an over, the fieldsmen changing to take up new positions, the happy visiting spin bowler taking the ball, tucking up his bowling-arm sleeves, licking anticipatory fingers. Pete spoke again, in the same low tone.

"Shouldn't be telling you all this, Billy'd have my guts. But— it's Tom. Isn't it? I thought maybe you'd—you know. Know something that might help. Living next door, Sally being matie with Julie. You saw a lot of him." No secret, that the families were on good terms, that Charlie and Tommy often arrived with their wives and the bab for cricket, sharing one car. Pete and his wife had often been to parties, they'd played bridge in one house or the other.

"I don't know anything, really, about his past," Charlie said.

"Never asked him. Well, you don't, do you? Did you come down specially?"

"No. Yes—I suppose I did. Billy said take a couple of hours off, get yourself a kip and a haircut, we've been working all night. Thought I'd just have a word. I miss you, you bugger. You know—the old days, chewing everything over. Did some good work, didn't we?"

"Mm." Detective Constable Wood, Detective Constable—and then Sergeant—Parsons. Until Pete loosened the connection by becoming Inspector Parsons, working above his oppo's normal sphere of operation; and Charlie, left behind and comparing progress, turned the whole thing in. And now Pete was chief inspector. "Do I keep my trap shut, or can I tell Sally?"

Pete hesitated. The spin bowler waved his close-in fielders to gather round the bat which Tony was tapping on the ground, facing up. "Yes. But *not* for the paper. Not yet. All right?"

"Right." More trust. The man was saying: She might know something without knowing she knows, come during confidences exchanged with Julie. Men do not question a friend, but women must find out all about each other. You know, he was saying, as a copper yourself the sort of thing I need. You will pass it on if you gather anything, discreetly. So that Billy the Fumer won't know I put you in the picture.

The bowler wheeled in, turned his arm over. A click from behind Tony's groping bat, a yellow bail in the air, fielders and the bowler leaping, howling their gleeful "ZA-A-AAT?" to the bright-blue sky. All the players on the field moving toward the pavilion, bringing their shadows with them.

"All out for thirty-eight," said Pete. "What a cockup. Wish I hadn't come. Well—back to the spinning wheel."

"I still put money on amnesia," Charlie said.

"Him *and* his bloody motor car? Let's hope you've got it right."

Notoriously, women are highly emotional creatures. Something to do with the menstrual cycle? Very probably. One thing is certain: You can never be sure how they will react to any given situation. The game was all over by four-thirty, and that is a full hour before the pub opens. So the players dispersed; the home team leaving sheepishly, unable to offer the visitors even the traditional beer session; the visitors more happily, a glorious victory under the belt but cheated of what some maintain is the best part of a cricket match. Charlie drove Sally home in near-silence, which she believed was due, on his part, to loser's chagrin, and he believed owed itself on hers to tea being served at the gallop, haphazardly and with floaters in the cup. Both were partly right.

He did not tell her about Tommy on the way. He waited until they were home, debating in his mind whether he should tell her at all. Perhaps he would not have done; but she said as she finished the just-home drink, "I hope we're eating out this evening."

"Of course we are," he said. They always did, on home-match Saturdays, usually driving into the country to a favourite small restaurant after the post-game beer.

"Then I hope you're not going to sulk all evening." There was irritability in her, due in part, no doubt, to the heat. It gets very warm in a cricket pavilion crammed with sweating male bodies, to whoever has to serve the teas in an unexpected and infuriating rush. The stress of the last few days, too, was telling upon her by now.

"I'm not sulking," Charlie said. "Why would I be sulking?" But it sounded as though he was. After all, he had his own stress.

"What else do you call it? I'm not having my evening spoiled just because you got walloped in a cricket match."

"It's got nothing to do with a cricket match."

"What has it got to do with, then?"

"It's Tommy," he said; and went on to tell her what Pete told him. She erupted with unexpected, explosive force.

"Rubbish. Bloody rubbish. I don't believe it."

There it is: the irrational reaction. A couple of days either side of this evening, she might have taken it quite differently; but to

63

add to her stresses, she was coming up to her period. Charlie said,

"Don't be daft. Why would Pete say it if it wasn't true?"

"Pete's not God," she cried. Her voice was rising. "He can make mistakes."

"It's not only Pete—it's Billy the Fumer—the Gloucester police—it's all in the records—"

"Who says so?"

"Pete."

"Pete!"

His voice was up, to contend with hers. "The police don't make mistakes—"

"You did, you made plenty in your day. What about when you locked up the drunk, and it turned out to be a heart attack?"

The pitch of his voice rose higher. Sore in him still, the time he picked up a recumbent drunk and had him locked in to sleep it off. The man was dead when they looked at him in the morning. That error counted against him, he firmly believed, in the promotion stakes. "Not in this sort of case I didn't."

"You never had this sort of case. You cocked up the little ones. You think because you never got up high enough to help, they don't make big cockups further up?"

"Don't take it out on me," he roared. She was whipping him cruelly.

"You're supposed to be his friend," she cried. "And so is bloody Pete!"

"All right—all right—you can soon find out if it's true, can't you? You work on a bloody paper—give the Gloucester rags a tinkle. They'll have it all on file."

"So I will, don't worry. First thing on Monday." And after a time: "It's shock. He's lost his memory."

And there you are. Another Saturday ruined. So much for the guarantee that the ability to knock each other out sexually automatically moulds two egos into one.

To anybody observing sympathetically, it would have been obvious that in her distress she was fending off desperately the acceptance of any criminal involvement by the husband, himself a friend, of a friend horribly dead. Shocks enough she had had. She would not even entertain the idea that his villainy was responsible for the disappearance of the man who sat hunched and shattered on her settee, who lay all night awake and suffering—she knew he did—in her guest bedroom.

Charlie, at present, was not observing sympathetically. "If it's amnesia," he said, his own professed belief in it suspended by his need to put her down, "what about his car? Has that got it, too? They haven't pulled that in, even."

"Car?" she said. "That's rich! Old Harry hasn't got his back yet, has he? That's really rich." He walked right into that one. Score it to her.

They worked it up into a very fair old row. Perhaps they both needed it to blow the top off stress, to pull their minds away from the tragedy and Tommy. Certainly, he never appeared again in the argument. They went for personal misattributes, and screwed it off in a different direction.

6

After the restaurant closed in the small hours of Sunday morning, it took considerable argument before Hans was persuaded that they must act now on their own. Mario had fear enough; but the big man by now had been brooding too long, and like many Germans when bereft of definite leadership and so not able to function within a known discipline, he piled fear upon fear until fear shaded into panic. He said,

"Ve must not go to it. Iss mad for us to go."

"We can't leave it where it is." Very little accent left in Mario now, his Neapolitan quaintness vanished with the last customer. This was not his first sojourn in England. "If the police are looking for Mr. Tommy, they are bound to visit the haulage depot, aren't they? They'll visit everywhere. You want them to find it standing there?"

"Vere *iss* Mr. Tommy?"

"Chrissakes—how do I know?" It had been the burden of the big man's terror-song for the last half hour, ever since the French chefs went home and Mario pulled down the blinds. Even during the afternoon break—the restaurant closed between three o'clock and six—when they went their separate ways, he had rung Mario at his flat to pose again this question to which nobody had the answer. "All I know is, if the police find it, we're right in it."

"Better poliss dan dem."

Had they known more about Tommy's emotional and criminal past, Mario, at least, the cooler, more professional one, might have considered as possibly responsible for bomb and disappearance people not related to their affair. Mario did know of Tommy's criminal record—he was well briefed before he arrived—but that was all he did know, the bare fact with no deeper details. And Hans knew nothing at all. There had never been any reason why Tommy should reveal to either intimate secrets from the past.

As it was, very naturally given the fact that all those engaged in nefarious enterprise grow more jumpy as involvement grows, fearing especially violence used as punishment for aberration, Hans believed implicitly and Mario almost as surely that the chicken was home to roost. But Mario, who had known prison in Italy, also feared the police, and deportation to face unforgiving men after a long term. There were solid reasons why he should not be shipped back to Italy a failure.

There were reasons, then, why the police must not set on to inquiries that must blow his life to pieces. And the others with power to do it—they must be persuaded that no aberration had taken place or ever been thought of. Not on his part. From no point of view could the cargo be allowed to fall into the hands of the police.

"Sit down," he said. "Have some coffee, it will steady you." There is always good coffee in restaurant kitchens staffed by Continentals. "And give me a cup. Now listen—we move it out—"

"Ve cannot—at this time—"

"Not now." Not at two o'clock on a Sunday morning. A car out at that time is a sitting duck for bored patrolmen looking for drivers with liquor on the breath or suspicious cargos aboard. Or for any other malevolent party. "Later—about eight. It will be light then." Risky—but better than leaving it until later still. The police do not sleep all day Sunday, and who knew at what time they might decide they had better take a look at Tommy's business premises?

"The airplane—"

"We do not look for the airplane, *stupido.*" The crafty plane from Italy would have come and gone.

"Vere do ve go, den?"

There was the crux of the matter. Mario did not know where to go. Tommy had fixed everything; he was the only direct contact man. Playing things very close to the chest—a wise precaution—any addresses he had, any phone number that Mario might have rung, had never been passed on. The man had simply vanished, leaving behind a terrible quandary. And new, pressing terror.

Who bombed Tommy, who had him now? Not the side he, Mario, was working for. The others, then? Or *their* opposition? Both were vicious, both fanatical. Both more than capable of killing them, all three. Given the chance, he might be able to concoct a story to explain away the missing of the delivery rendezvous, but who was to say that he would be given that chance? If they had found out—as he believed—if, even now, they were waiting only for him to reveal where the cargo was hidden—

But the van could not stay where it was. It had to be moved out of reach of the police, in spite of all the risks; and he knew of only one place where he might take it.

"We go to the city," he said.

"Vere in de city?"

"I'll tell you when we get there."

"I do not like," said Hans. "Iss nod possible—"

"Shut up, shut up, shut up," Mario said. "Shut up, or I'll kill you myself." He looked as though he might, using one of the long, razor-sharp kitchen knives.

At eight o'clock, more or less, the van nosed out from the garage and set off, taking a route through town suburbs that would bring it not onto the main trunk road leading directly to the city, but across and into lanes and the minor roads. A longer drive, but safer, Mario had decided. Village policemen, for one thing, are less likely to be abroad early on Sundays than are the

68

round-the-clock shifts on main roads controlled directly from town or city. And anybody dogging on behind is very plain to see, easier lost by a man who knows these byways. If they could be lost. Certainly, it was more of a bet than trying to outpace anything faster than the van on a broad, straight highway.

Another reason for taking this route: It came out eventually to where old abandoned warehouses stood alongside the canal on the edge of the city. Mario knew this blackened and lugubrious area too. They could approach it without touching the city proper, and among those decrepit warehouses where nobody went—why should they? Nothing but dank decay to be gained—there must be one—he thought he knew where there was one—where the van could be stashed. Not hidden properly; but at least stashed, wiped clean of prints and away from him. With the cargo off-loaded and hidden. Better to do that. Better.

Because if they came after him, he could at least say he did the best he could for them, having no way to make contact. He'd hidden the gear—they could collect it. He'd say—truthfully—that the business of Tommy had thrown everything, and he'd had to miss the rendezvous, and he couldn't get in touch, and he couldn't leave everything where the police would inevitably find it, now could he?

But even if he found, as he prayed he might, a safe hiding place for the dangerous cargo, the cargo that could get him twenty?—thirty?—forty?—years, or deportation and maybe a cut throat back in Italy, even then the problem was not properly taken care of. The van would have to vanish too. It was registered in Tommy Grover's name; if he simply abandoned it they'd trace it straight back. The police would.

So the whole van must disappear. But how?

First things first. Worry about that later—get away from the gear. Get it hidden—there must be cellars in those warehouses, there must be—ventilation systems, great pipes in which things could be stowed. Cellars—store rooms—there *must* be places. See to that first. Drains—manholes—there *must* be places.

Jesu Christos—what a nightmare it had all become—

Hans saw the car first, but by only a second. He had the advantage of the interior rear-view mirror, angled for him in the driver's seat. He sobbed, *"Achtung—mein Gott,"* like a U-boat crew in a wartime movie, when the avenging destroyer comes creaming. They were swinging off that necessary short stretch of main road into the network of lanes, and the wing mirror on Mario's side flashed it at once, a dark sedan coming in behind them.

"Keep going, keep going," he said, and reached under his arm for the automatic pistol. Useless, really—if it was them, whoever they were, they would undoubtedly be armed, and better than he was. They could gun him down, for sure. He could, perhaps, have shot out their front tyres, leaning out of the window as in American cop series, although this is not so easy as it looks. Truth is, he was not thinking the matter through clearly. He drew the gun simply because a man who may shortly be facing God-knows-what feels less naked with one in his hand.

No practical value, either, in his instruction to Hans. The big man had no intention of stopping, his foot was going down on the accelerator even before Mario spoke. A good driver, very good. A professional, able to handle anything from big long-distance rig down through racing car to mechanized bicycle and coax every ounce of performance from it. Took to it when he finished with boxing, and found a greater vocation. Even now, in his time of panic, he sent the van flying along the hedge-bordered lane. There were four men in that car, he could see them in his mirror.

No way for him or for Mario to know that they were very young men, no more than youths, driving a car borrowed from the father of the lad behind the wheel. No way they could overhear the conversation.

The lads had been to an all-night party, and not one of them should have been driving at all. There had been pot going round, and a deal of cheap liquor, grain and grape indiscriminately mixed. And they were young, the driver not more than eighteen. Bounding energy and staying power are the attributes of youth, not discretion in the use of wine, women, and song.

To give them their due, they might not have set out for home at this time but for the fact that the car was borrowed without Father's knowledge. It had to be there when he came out with Mother to go to church in it. They had meant to be on the road much earlier; but you know how it is, trying to get away from a still functioning teenage party. There are hairs of dog to swallow, people to be rounded up and corralled in the car—this one unravelled from his bird, that one shoved under the tap. There are dates to be made, there is kissing and fumbling taking longer than you thought it would. Women, the last man said as he slammed himself into the horn-honking car, are like paint. Stir 'em up, it takes a helluva time to get 'em off your hands. Nice line. Very man-of-the-world.

So at eight-fifteen on this bright Sunday morning they turned off the main road, right behind an unmarked Dodge van, taking the long way back to the city for much the same reason. They travelled these lanes often after parties, more usually in one of the bangers that came amongst them and were hammered unmercifully until sold off, or swapped, or gone kaput—none of them currently had one operative. Hence the borrowing—and they had never yet met a copper on a Sunday.

Young men always drive fast, and often are impelled to take issue with those who seem to challenge their cherished self-image as King of the Road. This young driver, having the Dodge ahead, at once laid down his foot, swinging out to roar past, with happy catcalls from his friends and a sticking up of two fingers, before they reached the point where the road narrowed and twisted, turning itself into a lane; and the van, instead of growing larger, stayed where it was. Even began to dwindle slightly, Hans' foot well down.

He was straightening out his corners, that bloke in the van, cutting them like racing drivers do, as can be seen any Saturday on telly. "Bloody liberty," the lad beside the car driver said. "He's taking you on, he's out to make a race of it. Get after him, Mike."

"Hang on," said Mike. He trod the accelerator flat to the floor, and Father's engine bellowed because there was a little hole in the silencer. And now, purely because no Dodge van, however well handled, can match a reasonable car on the run, he began to gain. But not fast enough, he wouldn't be up to overtake before that narrowing of the road. The bloke's unexpected accelerating had done him.

"Get him, Mike, get him!" his passengers chorused. One at least was still too liquor-woozy to know what was going on, who was there to be got, but he shouted anyway.

"You won't take him now," cried the lad in the passenger's seat as they swept into the narrowing lane. "Not without shoving him over the hedge."

"I'll get the bastard at the bridge," Mike swore; and all alive with catcalling and Red Indian whooping, the car raced on, able to maintain position—even, by virtue of its easier handling qualities, creeping up until it clung to the Dodge's tail; but quite unable to pass.

If the Dodge van has a fault, it lies where it lies with any similar vehicle: The interior becomes noisy when the engine, seated back between driver and passenger, is brought under power. But for this and the fact that exterior noise coming from the rear tends to whirl away in the slipstream, Mario might have heard that catcalling and readjusted his thinking. He might have pointed out to Hans the self-evident fact that men, come to get them, would not come yipping Apache war-cries. They would work in grim silence. Hans might even have listened to him and pulled aside into one of the passing places or a recess fronting a farm gate, to let the idiots go by, afterwards proceeding in less hectic fashion, untroubled to journey's end. But only the noise of the engine and the skreek of tyres on the sharper bends could be heard in the cab.

They could see, though—they could see that car coming up with intent to their tail. Mario tightened his grip on his pistol, Hans applied his desperate skills. The Dodge shot on, with the car behind close enough now to have been attached on a tow-rope.

It was everybody's luck that a PC Wooderson was thinking of buying a cottage out this way, and bored with no business on main-road early patrol had suggested to his patrol mate, PC Eddie Pringle, that they detour, take half an hour; he'd like to know what he thought of it. People do love to show friends the house they are thinking of moving into.

Well, Eddie Pringle didn't mind, he was as bored with cruising up and down as was PC Wooderson. It was a tedious shift, any one is that laps over into Sunday morning. No fun at all. Nothing ever happens outside the town. Not much happens inside it until the pubs turn out in the afternoon.

They had seen the cottage and were in the lane running along the bottom of Hanger Hill, on the way back to the beat, when they heard the roar of fast-moving engines and an exuberant yipping. It was coming along the lane they must shortly join. "Hallo-allo," said PC Wooderson. "What's that, then?" And the truck shot by, with the car bellowing through its little silencer hole, loud with the cowboy-and-Indian cacophony and too close for safety. The truck made a perfect racing gear-change, setting itself at the hill.

"What the bloody hell's going on there?" said PC Eddie Pringle.

"Start the light flashing," his driving oppo said. They were up to the end of this byway now and he was swinging over to turn left, instead of making the right turn back towards the main road.

"Going after them, then?"

"Can't just let 'em go belting about like that, can we? Wouldn't mind betting they're all pissed."

"We could fall in the shit; we're supposed to be patrolling the beat."

"Bollicks, we could. Say we chased 'em all the way from the main road, don't we?" Constable Wooderson, another good driver and happily anticipating the chance to use his talent, sent the black-and-white car at the hill in the wake of the others. Some distance to make up, but he had the best vehicle. He also had a siren. His mate set it going as they swept upward, the pursued cars visible only as often as the twisting lane allowed. And it does twist, up that hill.

Hanger Hill is the well-known beauty spot, very popular with picnickers but not soon after eight on a Sunday morning. Both the leading cars heard that siren, and both drivers caught a flash of the sudden police car not far behind. Mario saw it too in his wing mirror as Hans, choking, kept his foot hard down. In his father's car, Mike said,

"Christ! Sodding coppers!"

"Oo, bloody hell," said his mate. Those in the back cacophonized unaware, too high on all-night liquor and the sheer exhilaration of rushing through this bright young morning to care what was happening.

Innocent drivers pull over when a police siren shrieks behind them. They let the car through, they stop if bidden. No good trying to get away: You can't shake off a good police driver, and even if you do, there is a number plate tacked to the back of your motor. But no innocent driver was here, excepting always the policeman. With that load aboard and police now added to the terror on his tail, Hans never gave a thought to stopping. True, to say that he was no longer able to give coherent thought to anything at all. As for Mike—

This was his father's car. Get nobbled, the old man'd go hairless. Get nobbled still half-cut, all your mates pissed and hollering in with you— And a bit of pot about— And you buzzing some bastard in a van— Christ!

Liquor alone clouds judgement, and even sober young drivers again and again overestimate their ability. He realized, Mike did, that he had a number plate at the back. Noted, even if he got away, it would bring the police to his very father. He believed the police, hampered by bends and distance, could not have read it yet. He must get past the van—get it between him and them—shoot off, perhaps, down a side lane—he didn't know what. Get past, was the thing—where he had meant to—where the road widened—now—

They were over the brow of the hill, on the steep drop-run round the last bend before the road widens, shooting down to the bridge. As they came onto the widening he trod hard and swung the wheel, racing to get alongside—alongside and clear—

There wasn't room, of course. Silly young bugger. Hans saw him come up, and Hans' driving by now was not of his impeccable best. But his grown-up experience knew what had to happen, no way at all to prevent it. Sobbing, he twitched the wheel and ploughed straight into the nearside parapet of the bridge while the other car smashed into the offside, tipping over, tumbling in a smashing of glass, rending of metal, Indian yips changed to screaming, into the river Elver flowing peacefully through the valley.

The police heard it, but did not see it go because they were not yet out from the bend. Hans neither saw nor heard it; he was slashed by the shattering windscreen and unconscious. Mario was aware of chaos without detail. His door had burst open and he had been hurled through it, out among nettles to roll half-stunned down the river bank—which was what saved him, shielding him from the blast and flying metal.

A crashed car seldom burns, except in Hollywood cops-and-robbers, when they need the effect. A tumbling ball of fire photographs so well. In reality, smashing the engine cuts the pump, so that no more volatile fuel is fed through. But flamers do happen, usually if the engine has been worked hard and the smash breaks the joint between fuel pipe and carburetor, dropping petrol onto the red-hot manifold. A flash-back then and she'll burn, all right.

This is what happened here. Without fire the cargo would not have exploded, because none of it was primed. But a flash of fire was enough.

The police came round the bend just as it all went up, a tremendous flash, a roar, a blasting shock that shattered the squad car windscreen as PC Wooderson trod hard on the brake, rending van and Hans to flaming pieces, leaving only wheels on fire and smoking under-chassis crumple-nosed against the shattered parapet of the bridge; flinging glass and metal high into the air.

"Jesus Christ!" said PC Wooderson, sleeves cut but physically unharmed because somehow he had raised his arms before his face. He sat bolt-eyed in a state of shock; and beside him his mate, blood coming through the torn hands covering his face, sobbed a repeated scream: "I'm blind—I'm blind—I'm blind—"

7

They spent an unpleasant Saturday evening, Charlie and Sally, and an equally unhappy night. Pity, in such lovely weather. He took her out to dinner, not to the Belle Epoque because it was too hot in town, but to a place they went to often in the country, where in the rare fine spells of an English summer tables were set in the lawn under fairy lamps. The beauty of the night should have soothed them, but the quarrel lingered. They drove home in frigid silence and went to bed, where they lay isolated, each well over to his own side.

On Sunday, when Charlie came from the bathroom fragrant with bath-oil and after-shave and dabbed with a deodorant sworn to on television by a well-beloved ex-heavyweight boxer, to join Sally in the kitchen where she stood with her hair tied back with a ribbon, wearing her dressing gown while she fried bacon and eggs, she broke the sulking silence for the first time since they coldly wished each other a good night, not meaning a word of it.

"Are you going to ring Pete?"

"What for?" said Charlie.

"I should think it's obvious. He may have found Tommy."

"He won't have. He'll ring us, when he does."

"If he bothers." She managed to suggest in the cold tone that neither he nor Pete was particularly interested in the matter. Quarrelling women do this, when their emotional logic has them lumping together resentment against husband and friend, whom they see as standing in cahoots on the opposite side of an issue. And men rise always, like pike. Charlie snapped.

"Look—I'm not ringing Pete every five minutes, he's got enough to do without me cackling in his ear all the time like a bloody hen."

It was enough. She was emotionally strung up with grief and worry and reaction by quarrelling, and all this heightened by premenstrual tension. She slammed down the spatula used in her kitchen for flicking bubbling fat over frying eggs and turning bacon over, and said, "Then *I'll* ring him. If you don't want a burned breakfast, you can do it yourself."

He thought, anger savaging up in him again: Let the bloody lot burn. Almost, he stalked out and left it; but fat goes on fire, and there'd been enough of fire lately. Also, the only way he could stalk, unless he unbolted the back door—and the act of unbolting destroys the stalk almost as much as coming back for your hat— was after her, into the hall. It would have looked ridiculous, their both stalking in the same direction, so he picked up the spatula. Oh, he was quite capable of frying his own bloody egg, she needn't worry about that.

He could hear her dialling and waiting. He could hear her end of the conversation. She was saying:

"Pete? Morning. Sally. Fine, thanks. You? Good. We were just wondering—anything about Tommy? Oh. Uh-huh. No, of course I haven't told the paper, Charlie said you said don't. Don't be bloody patronizing." He'd probably said, "Good girl," or something. "Yes. All right. Bye." And she rang off without even sending love to Suzie, the plump and comely wife.

Charlie lifted out the bacon and said in his head, "Sod it," when his lifting spatula broke the egg yolk. She came back into the kitchen. After a minute, he said, "What did he say?"

"Nothing."

"Don't be daft, I heard you talking."

"He's *heard* nothing, they've *found* nothing. He said he'll ring us if anything comes in."

"That," said Charlie, "is what I bloody well said in the first place."

78

The man came down to the cellar when church bells were pealing. They could not be heard from here. Nothing could be heard from here until the screek of the bolts, grate of the lock, click of switch that made Tommy screw up his eyes against the sudden flood of light from a bare bulb. He was going to die, and he knew it, but fear of death diminished before the increasing agony of raging thirst.

The man carried a mug of water. He approached, put the mug down carefully, and said, "I am going to let you have a little drink. Nobody will hear you, you can scream or shout as loud as you like when I ungag you. But *I* shall hear you, and I don't like loud noises. So I shall probably pour the water all over the floor."

He moved to within arm's reach, and leaned across to peel off the Elastoplast still fastened over Tommy's mouth. His nose wrinkled. "Phoo," he said, "you do stink. Nature won't be denied, will she? Good job I haven't been feeding you, you'd have stunk the whole house out by now. It's quite fresh upstairs. Now—this is going to hurt, I'm happy to say, you've grown quite a beard." And he ripped away the plaster. Tommy hardly felt the agony, all his soul was fixed on that mug.

The man seated himself on a little stool beside the flock mattress, wet and stained and stinking now. He had sat there many times since he brought Tommy in—how many days ago Tommy didn't know—so that he could taunt in some degree of comfort. This was the first time he had appeared with water, and he was in no hurry to administer it. He picked up the mug, cradled it between his hands, and said smilingly,

"I don't suppose you thought you'd ever see any of this again, did you?" He raised the mug to his own lips, took a sip. Tommy's agonized eyes reached out for the cup. It seemed to be brimming. He made a cracked mewing noise. The man said,

"Well, I've been reading it up, you see. Homo sapiens can survive without water under normal conditions for between one and two weeks. That's not very long, is it? Unless I decide to do something else—burn you alive, perhaps, or cut your penis off—not a very appetizing task, the state you're in, but I suppose one could wear rubber gloves—I want you to last longer than that. And now I look at you, I don't think you'd have lasted much longer, not even for a week. That'll be the gag, I suppose, it will dry the saliva up. Do you think that's it? And perhaps lying in one position doesn't help." He took another sip from the mug.

Lying in one position had been part of the agony, particularly at first—how long? without light, time has no divisions—when he could squirm, at least, to seek ease from cramps; but by now he could hardly move at all, his muscles were locking; and that particular aspect of agony muted as the raging agony of thirst grew. His throat moved convulsively, his dry tongue flicked over dry lips, his eyes followed the mug.

"So I think we'll give you a drink, say, every two or three days," the man was saying. "Just enough to sustain life. That way, we might be able to make it last for weeks. You'll like that, won't you?"

He smiled upon Tommy; not expecting answers, not wanting any. Enjoying himself, that's all. From the state of Tommy's tongue and lips, probably he could not have answered anyway with more than a croak.

"Two or three days may turn out to be a bit liberal," the man said. "But then again, it may not. We'll just have to play it by ear, we may find a spoonful a day is best. Or perhaps as you get used to it we can increase the time between—every fourth day, every fifth perhaps. It will be interesting, to see how it all works out. I dare say you're getting impatient for a drop right now, aren't you?" He moved. "Come on, then—let's lift your shoulders up, we don't want it all running down your neck, do we?"

He put his arm round Tommy's shoulders to raise him up, his nose exaggeratedly averted. "God," he said, "what had you been eating? You're worse than a French latrine." He tilted the mug against cracked, stubbled lips.

Tommy was not hearing, he was gulping—gulping—; twice

only. The mug was almost empty. The man took it away from the desperately reaching mouth, his smile widening now, his voice a chuckle. "I'll bet you thought it was full, didn't you? I was only pretending to sip—look—that's all we have left." And he tipped the mug, to let the last precious swallow trickle onto the ground.

Now he released Tommy's shoulders, so that he sagged again on the mattress. Went back to his stool and sat for a while in silence, the smile still playing on his lips, his eyes alight with pleasure. For some time he stayed, enjoying himself. Then he said,

"You know, there's a great sexual element in this. Not that I intend to sodomize you or anything, nothing like that, don't worry. I'd need to be really perverted for that, wouldn't I, the state you're in? I mean the power. There's nothing I can't do to you, is there? Castrate you—anything. I was thinking of that in bed this morning, and I found myself with an enormous erection. Would have pleased the wife no end. If I had a wife."

He picked up the mug. "Well—I'll leave you in peace now. I don't think we need the gag anymore, you can yell all you want to, really. I'll be down again, later. Or tomorrow, I may put it back then, depends how I feel. Try to restrain yourself, you stink enough already."

Pete Parsons did not become connected to the crash and explosion at the bridge close by the village of Wenden Stavely until the afternoon. Sally, ringing that morning, guided perhaps by raw intuition rather than by sober reasoning, caught him just as he was leaving for the station. Even a policeman, unless summoned, does not rush in for duty on a Sunday morning. The station knows where to ring him. Nobody seriously nit-picks at a CID man's working hours. Unless he is strongly self-motivated he doesn't last in the job.

Today, his physical presence was not needed at all. All the seeking, inquiring visiting was being conducted by other people, there was nothing he, or Detective Chief Superintendent Billy the Fumer Fumery, or the Chief Constable himself, could get any kind of grip on until one or all of the sought men or some other lead came in. But he went to the station anyway. Too much disturbance in his mind, all churning around his friend and things connected with him, to permit any enjoyment even in a long lie-in softened by a plump and comely wife.

He took one hour, and then he got up, showered, shaved, dressed, took Sally's call, and left Suzie there with two biscuits and a cup of coffee. She said did he want any breakfast? He said he could get something in the canteen. CID wives who do not fancy the divorce court learn to tolerate peculiar domestic arrangements. She knew what was nagging at him, and the Grovers were her friends, too. Even cheated of her cherished Sunday morning nookie her lips were soft and warm when she kissed him goodbye. They'd make it up, when he got a day off in lieu of.

When he does come into the office, a ranking detective finds no shortage of work. He hands over much of his current load as he is assigned to a sudden major case, particularly where murder is involved; but there is always over-spill, there are cases bubbling on, and he the only man knowing all the form. The men taking on his other work need to know things, they send in typed reports, copy to him. Other crime does not hang there in a state of suspense, patiently waiting until he gets back from his murder case.

So he spent a fairly busy morning and went home to lunch, because it was Sunday. Had ham-and-tongue and egg salad, chilled fruit mixed up in a bowl with ice cream, and a little cold beer—it was still bloody hot, as his agreeable wife agreed. Then he kissed her again, caressed one breast briefly while he made randy-animal growls at her, because she really was very worthy when she discarded all but hot-weather minimum and walked about with her wiggle and her soft vibrations. And then he went back to the station.

Half an hour later, Billy the Fumer rang from his own office. He, too, had been in all morning, suffering as Pete was from sheer detective's frustration. And what is true of a chief inspector is certainly true of a chief superintendent: There is always plenty of work to keep the mind moving. He said,

"Pete—that crash at the bridge. You heard about it?"

"Uh-huh." Everybody had heard about it; and not only here, but all over the country where people bent an ear to radio or cocked an eye to television. Four lads killed in a car—van and presumably occupants blown to bits by mysterious explosion—a copper blinded—you don't get raw meat every day, do you?

"The van's been traced, they found a number plate."

"That's bloody quick, isn't it? On a Sunday?" The Swansea licensing centre, through which most vehicles are traced, closes from Friday to Monday.

"Not everybody sits on their arse on Sundays. The Swansea police will have raked somebody out of bed." Easy enough, really, when the police stomp along demanding instant action or a call to the Home Office, whichever the bald little man prefers. "Point is, it's down to your mate."

"My mate?"

"Grover. Tommy Grover. He's down as owning it."

"Bleeding hooray."

"Yes, that's what I said. They just passed it on to me. Come up, will you?"

Up went Pete to a better office than his. Bigger, with brighter walls, better carpet, and a free-standing hat-rack. Such things go by rank. The air conditioning worked better in here, too. Augmenting it, the Superintendent wafted a miniature battery-powered hand-fan about his heavy features, sitting at the desk with the telephone held to his ear. "Uh-huh," he said. "Yes. Thank you, Mr. Phillips. Uh-huh. Goodbye." He put the phone down and addressed Pete. "Dodge van, the Swansea fellows say. Registration number SYG 248 X. That was Mr. Phillips; I expect you know him."

"Who is he?"

"Manager of your man Grover's haulage firm. Hasn't got a

83

Dodge on the books, all his stuff's heavy transport. Doesn't know a thing about it, says our boy didn't keep it there."

"Uh-huh." Say it for Billy: Once a crack appeared, he was in at once with a crowbar. All the volcanic energy that manifested itself at times of frustration as short-fuse fuming transformed to immediate action. The man Phillips would have been on his list already, as one who knew Tommy. Not bad, though, to have belled him at home so soon.

"There's a pistol, too, found near the van, the main blast missed it. Beretta 45. What do you think about that?"

"Dabs on it?"

"All the grip's burned off. It's in Forensic. They may dust something up, but I doubt it, it's pretty bashed about."

"Who was driving? Do we know?"

"We do not. Blown to buggery, whoever he was. Little charred shreds, we don't know which little bits are him yet. Tell you this: He was carrying explosives."

Told about the bang this morning, Pete had immediately concluded—any policeman would—that the van had not exploded due to a load of chickens in the back. Explosives going bang on the public highway travelling in a small van—automatically, it had to be a major case. But nothing, he had thought, to do with him. Nothing to do with Tommy. He said now, as the possibility struck home,

"Could have been Tommy Grover. The driver."

"Could have been. Could have been Ken Dodd, for all we know; it's beginning to look funny enough."

"Mm," said Pete. He could think of nothing else to say. The Fumer was speaking straight on, anyway.

"Suggest we get out there, take a look at it. The Vauxhall's been heaved out of the river and the squad car's back. I've radioed, told 'em not to move anything else. The Old Man knows, I've been on to him. He'll meet us there." The Old Man, in any police force, is the Chief Constable or the Commander or whoever is right on top of the totem. The title is invariable; just as is the Guv'nor for the man leading a major inquiry. This was the Guv'nor, this big and heavy man switching off his little whirling fan and rising from his desk. He looked it, too. Not every guv'nor does.

They drove through the unusual heat, finding when they got to the bridge the Chief Constable already here. Presumably in deference to his own hierarchic position he wore the jacket of his dark suit, the only man here not down to shirt sleeves. He stood with a group of lesser men, some uniform and some plain clothes, surveying the general mayhem.

By one of the unpredictable quirks to which it is subject, the blast had all gone outward and upward. So the black and twisted chassis of the van stood where it stopped on impact; but most of the parapet was gone, jumbled now on the river bank or sunk in the river itself. The hedges on either side of the road had suffered and a chestnut tree that stretched its boughs right above the vehicle was shattered and black and bald, scarred forever by the flash of fire, all its leaves gone or withered.

But there was no crater, not much damage to the road itself or the surrounding grass, if you except the area of surface burn immediately around the wreck. The other car, looking not too badly damaged, had been hauled by tractor out of the river by now, and the lads drowned inside it taken away. The police car was gone, and the policemen with it. Other cars were there now, among them Tony Scully's small fire wagon. Tony himself stood among the group, towering above even the Chief Constable. And he was no dwarf.

"Ah," said the Chief, as the new arrivals came up. "You made it, then, Mr. Fumery." He was not being sarcastic, although he knew well how to be. It was just something said to greet them. "Strange business, what?"

"From what I've heard about it, sir," the Superintendent said, "very strange." High rank can admit to the very top brass, even in a police force, that it is not in possession of all the facts.

The Chief Constable filled in possible gaps. "Our driver says

85

the car with the lads in seemed to be buzzing this one; he thought they were drunk or high, the autopsy will tell us. When he went after them they appeared to want to run for it. Tried to get past the van, bounced off the bridge into the river, van hit the bridge and *boom.*"

This much the Superintendent knew. He said, "Explosives."

"Explosives." The Chief glanced at the fireman.

"Not much doubt about it," Tony Scully said. "Fuel flash-back wouldn't do it."

"So what do you think about that?" the Chief asked.

"Gang? Bank vaults—stock of gelly?"

"It'd take a fair whack of gelignite to do that." The Chief knew about these things, he was an old army man. Had a picture on his desk of his young self in sand boots.

"Maybe they'd bought in bulk, to store it."

Pete spoke up. He did not like what he was thinking, but it had to be thought. The others, no doubt, were thinking it too. "Terrorist mob? IRA? Provos?"

"Could be. Makes a funny feller out of your man Grover, Mr. Fumery, if the van belonged to him."

"Very funny, sir," the Super said. "Especially if he was driving."

"Mm. Well—it's down to the Special Branch now; they're sending somebody."

"Complicates matters, doesn't it?"

"They won't complicate us, they're very smart men."

"I didn't mean that, sir." Pressmen were here, too, snapping away happily. "I mean we've got all these people looking for possible kidnappers and the man Grover." The Superintendent indicated the Dodge chassis. "If that was Grover—we're using up an awful lot of overtime."

A very good point. Pete had reached it already, and the Chief saw it at once. "Mm," he said. "Mmm." Because if Grover went up with the van he wasn't kidnapped, was he? For reasons of his own, centred no doubt on the explosives, he had gone to earth, emerging to run the cargo out. Out of the country, himself with it? Whatever he had intended, if he blew up here there was no kidnapper or nappers. There was a fire-bomber—but if he was mixed up with gangs, criminal or terrorist, the two men being sought probably had nothing to do with it. Nor had a protection mob.

The Superintendent looked around. Up on the sunny hill were groups of people kept from coming closer by a couple of shirt-sleeved policemen—early holiday-makers and local residents, rubbernecking. "Have there been any ammo dumps raided lately?" he said. "I don't remember any."

Pete spoke again. "Doesn't have to be lately. They—he—could have stashed it. Drawn upon it when needed. This didn't have to be the first run."

"True. True. Properly stored, one good raid and they'd have stock for years. Get on to that when we get back, see who did what and when."

"Right."

"Wasn't there a raid at Bovey Tracey, year or so ago?" Tony Scully put in. "I seem to remember it."

"Mm. I believe there was." The Superintendent glanced at the Chief Constable. "We'll poke about a bit here, sir, but I doubt if it'll do us any good. How about our two lads?"

"The driver's all right," said the Chief. "Seems to have escaped it, shock and a few cuts. I'm afraid the other lad's blinded."

"Mm. Uh-huh. Can't think how they hadn't caught these her-berts earlier, presumably they chased them from the main road. Well—come on, Pete—let's see what's about. Then it's back to the drawing board, do a bit of new thinking."

Up on the hill a camera crew grunted with satisfaction and took footage of the investigating detectives peering at the chassis, the waterlogged Vauxhall, and all round about, the perspectives distorted by the telescopic lens, which gives lie forever to the naïve belief that the camera cannot lie. They would all be on telly tonight, looking mighty odd but recognizable.

It was the television news in the early evening that sprang the new matter on Charlie and Sally. They had passed the day as well as could be expected, even venturing into the garden with a book each, the loungers and a jug of gin-laced lemonade, to lie about in sun-bathing minimum; but the next-door ruin drove them away, so they went instead into the country, where Charlie found a little cricket to look at and Sally went walkabout, all through woods until she could paddle her feet in a stream. She enjoyed that, but altogether it was not one of their better days. In addition to the stress of fret and ill temper, the heat was becoming trying.

They were no longer actively quarrelling, but that unhappy aftermath was upon them, the condition in which two people can find little to say to each other. Again they drove home in near-silence, and when they came in Charlie switched the television on to catch the news.

A cloudburst in Somerset, volcanic eruption in Chile, the usual murders in Northern Ireland, the exploding car near Wenden Stavely, all introduced by a toothy lady with a West Kensington accent; and suddenly there was Pete, with Billy the Fumer and another man in a blue suit, poking about among the wreckage. He called to Sally doing things with tomato and lettuce in the kitchen.

"Hey—Pete's on telly. With Billy the Fumer. And the Old Man."

Sally came hurrying. It is not every day one's friends appear on telly. "What's he doing there?" she said. Meaning Pete, of course.

"There's been a crash," he told her. "At the bridge just before you get to Wenden Stavely. Van exploded. They must have put him on it. Him and Billy."

"On a car crash? In the middle of the Tommy business? Do they do that?"

"No," he said. "Not usually. Four lads drowned, van driver killed, and two coppers hurt."

The television lady was saying urbanely, as though explaining a knitting pattern to a rather dim ladies guild: ". . . police believe the van to have been carrying explosives. Princess Anne fell from her horse today during . . ." Pete was gone. Princess Anne was there now, picking herself out of a water jump and saying something naughty to a horse. Deaf viewers lip-reading must have had a nasty shock.

"Explosives," Charlie said. "That could explain it. They must reckon it big—Billy was there—even the Old Man."

"I'd have thought," said Sally, easier now, the unexpected happening banishing for a while that awkward tension between them, "they'd got enough to do, without fiddling about with other things."

"If it is other things." Charlie's police mind was working. "It might not be. It might tie in with Tommy."

"They didn't mention Tommy."

"Her Highness," the television lady said reassuringly, "was unhurt." The nation let out its suspended breath, giving thanks to God.

"Wouldn't know, would they? If there's a connection, Billy'll sit on it; he won't release it as news, probably."

"What connection?"

"I don't know, do I? All I know is what was on the box."

"The Ministry of Agriculture and Fisheries announced yesterday that the prolonged heat-wave could lead to increases in the price of root vegetables," the television lady cooed. "But a spokesman said that at this moment in time, the situation is not irreversible at the grass roots."

"I wonder if Pete's back yet. I might give him a ring."

Sally did not say, "How can he be back, we've just been watching him on telly?" Everybody knows news items are filmed. The basic rapport was re-establishing, both had embraced professions where natural curiosity is fostered and encouraged into nose for news, nose for the fishy smell. She said, "I would. I'd ring. If I were him, I'd expect it." This, perhaps, more than sexual compatibility, was what held them together: this closeness of understanding and interest, the fact that each could bring under discussion matters engaging their professional curiosity, sure of the other's interest.

"Mm," said Charlie. "I think I will."

Pete was not at the station, the WPC on switchboard duty said. Nor was he at home; his plump and comely Suzie said he rang earlier to tell her he would be late. Yes, she saw him on the box, but it made his face all salmon-pink. Charlie said on their set he tended toward yellow, rather, and yes, he'd give her love to Sally. Which he did, with his report, when he hung up.

"Wonder if the office will know anything?" she said, and took the phone over to try.

They had covered the story, of course. Bertie Fowler did it, but he'd gone home. They read his copy to her. Nothing in it about Tommy, no mention at all. And she said nothing. After all, only the antennae were concerned, she had no reason to start bunnies running. Not even a bunny to run. The only nose twitching was her own. And Charlie's, of course. She thanked them, and put the phone back into its fancy cradle. "Bertie Fowler covered it," she said. "Gone home. Nasty crash. But he doesn't mention anything else, not even Pete and Billy Fumery and the Chief."

"Mm," said Charlie.

"Mind you, that doesn't mean anything. If we got the story early he'd have skated over there; he could have been finished and gone before they arrived. I was speaking to Pete at ten; he hadn't even left home."

"And the crash was early. Means Pete and Billy got it later. So something's up, or they wouldn't have. Tell you who might know something—Tony Scully."

"Tony? Why Tony?"

"Fire Brigade business, isn't it? Explosion."

90

"Is it? I don't know."

"No harm in finding out. Let's have a bash."

Tony was at home. He said, "Yes, I was there. But I didn't get a chance to talk to Pete. The big brass was with him."

"Did they say anything about old Tom?" Charlie asked.

"Look," said Tony, "I can't go passing all the bits and pieces on, can I?"

"No, I know that, but—he's a mate, isn't he? And we're not going to go rushing out to tell the neighbours. Why did they all turn out, Pete and Billy Fumery and the Old Man?"

"Sorry, mate—can't say a dicky-bird. Official Secrets Act—I'd find myself on top of a ladder again, squirting water. Sal all right?"

"Yes, she's fine. Worried, of course, about Tommy."

"We all are, ain't we? Good gal, our Sal. Give her my love. See you, mate." And that was that.

"What did he say?" asked Sally.

"Nothing. Sweet Fanny. But something's up—he was backing away. Said the Official Secrets lark'd have him if he passed the bits on. I know old Tony. If nothing was funny at all he'd have said so, no messing. Why wouldn't he?"

"Why don't we go over?"

"Over where?"

"Wenden Stavely. Pete might still be there."

"Place will be crowded with bloody rubbernecks."

"All right, so we come back. No harm in it; it'll get us out of this place for an hour." And you *might*, her mind was telling herself, pick up a story. Maybe for the column—maybe something more lurid that you can have typed and ready, a genuine scoop, with a flying start when and if the police release—whatever it is. If it is anything.

"What about grub?" said Charlie. Not because he cared much about it, but because he needed a second or two to mull over whether it was a good idea or not, going out to Wenden Stavely.

91

"Oh hell—what are you, a tapeworm? We can shove a bit of lettuce in the car."

Sliced bread, ignoring the cotton-wooliness and lack of a bite-able crust, has its advantage: You can butter it and cram lettuce, tomato, and slices of ham between it, and have it plastic-bagged and into the car in less time than it took in the bad old days even to cut real bread. Three, four minutes, and they were turning out of the drive, en route for Wenden Stavely. But they did not see Pete there. He was on his way to the city, to pick up Clifton Parry. That's right—Julie's first husband.

Plenty of rubbernecks here. The hill was crowded, and a stream of cars was going into the lane from the main road end, being waved to turn round at a farmyard, hard-standing long before it got to the bridge, and directed out again by sweaty but determined policemen. It went back to the main road cursing and swearing it would write to the papers because—sod it—this was a free country; passing its own tail, still coming in. Meeting this two-way stream, Charlie said,

"See? Bloody rubbernecks. I told you so. They're keeping 'em out."

"All right—we turn round. Go through the Stipperton lane."

Another trait they had in common: Both hated not to reach the place they set out for. On holidays, they had trudged through mud and miles of brambles to get to a point that looked easy enough on the map. Natural tenacity is a prime requisite for press and policepersons both. So now they turned the car, drove a mile along the road, and turned off into a lane that only locals and those familiar with the area would realize led in toward where they wanted to go.

Whether the police on the spot would allow them to stay was a moot point. Both rather thought they would, even if Pete had left; Sally with confidence in the charm that seldom failed when she exercised it professionally, especially on junior-ranking men; Charlie because the very top brass would be away by now, and

Pete (and junior rank in general—he knew them all and they knew him) looked upon him still almost as one of themselves. Because the police necessarily exist in some degree of social isolation—the hours do it, and the very fact that they are copper, and set apart—loyalty between them runs deep.

To get to the bridge you must leave the car at a farm gate in this lane, just after it passes through the lost and lovely hamlet of Stipperton. You go through the farmyard—the frenzied dog won't hurt you—and by the footpath across a field, over a stile, and so to the river bank. Now you have a mile to cover, all beautiful, all easy walking along the towpath. Here and there the path is a bit overgrown, because few people know of this walk; being tucked away from the main motor roads, it is not marked on the tourist maps, but this will not impede you, it is only grass.

They pulled the car well over into the inlet by the farm gate to leave room for others to go by, and came forth, two good-looking people in evening sunlight; and if they did not pay full attention to the landscape as it deserved, this was because humanity walks through life always caught in its own affairs. So although they drew each other's attention now and again to items of extreme beauty, their talk was mostly of Tommy, and Pete, and the matter in hand. Until they came in half a mile to the old sheep pen, where Sally said,

"Hang on a minute."

Every man with experience of walking in the country with a woman knows that at some point she will disappear into the bushes, as he will himself turn aside. Difference is, woman will seek better concealment, being cursed by greater brain-washing and the resultant conviction that behind every tree lurks a dirty old man who, at a flash of nates and knickers to the knee, will leap out slavering to rape her. And yet even today the most liberated, if they be married at all, will rarely squat in the presence of husband, where safety may be expected to lie. Still they take to the woods.

So Sally stepped off the path, making by instinct for the old

93

dry-stone-walled sheep pen with the saggy open-fronted timber shelter. A wall offers greater concealment than a bush.

Through the gap she went where the gate used to be, and saw it immediately: a man's body, lying on its back under the shelter. She thought at first that it was a tramp sleeping, and was about to retreat to find a bush after all; but the well-pressed slacks and T-shirt, grass- and mud-stained though they were, looked wrong for a tramp. So was the neatly glossy black hair, and the face, in spite of stubble. He'd been hurt—there was a mess of dried blood on the forehead—and he wasn't asleep. Was he—with his arms thrown wide?

She moved closer; and then she recognized him and stepped back, to call over the wall. "Charlie—it's Mario."

Charlie, skating stones on the river, paused to call back. "What's Mario?"

"I've found him. In here."

"What are you talking about? Who says he's lost?"

"He's in here," she said. "Don't muck about—come and have a look."

Charlie came and said, "Well, I'll be buggered." He bent over Mario, checking for a pulse. Sally said,

"Not . . . dead, is he?"

"Pulse is there," Charlie told her. "Bit faint. Looks as if he's had a bang on the head. What's he doing here, for Christ's sake?"

"Never mind that—we'll have to get an ambulance."

"Yes." He stood up. "He's a bit cold. Haven't got a coat to put over him, have we? You stay with him—don't move him, we don't know what his injuries are. Shove something under his head. I'll sprint back—they'll have a phone at the farm."

"Hang on, hang on," Sally cried urgently. And even now, with one unconscious and the other a husband who for five years had crooned delight over every nook and cranny of her, she rushed out of the walled enclosure where men were, making for a nearby bush.

94

8

When Detective Chief Inspector Pete Parsons came into the station with the man who used to be Julie Grover's husband, he said to the sergeant in Reception who entered the arrival in a big black book: "Give Mr. Fumery a buzz, will you, George? Tell him I'm back." He then ushered the man wanted for questioning into one of the little spartan interview rooms and said, "Sit down, Mr. Parry, will you? No—not at the desk, on the other chair. Chief Superintendent Fumery will be here in a moment."

The man, smiling pleasantly, took the chair fronting the bare deal desk with a matching inadequate wooden chair behind it. No other furniture whatsoever; an interview room is meant to unsettle and not to give comfort. "Chief Superintendent, eh?" he said. "Must be something pretty important." A pleasant-seeming man altogether, tall and thin, with a face too chubby to fit the thinness. Receding, fluffy fair hair, light-blue eyes, and this pleasant smile. Nothing obviously mad showing, unless it was the air of enjoying everything happening to and around him.

"It is, sir, rather. The DCS will put you in the picture."

"DCS," the man murmured softly, as if to himself. "Jargon. Yes. Fascinating."

Chief Superintendent Fumery arrived now, at just about the time when Sally and Charlie bent over the body of Mario. He had been home once, and speeded back by a call from Pete saying he was on the way to the city, to pick up Clifton Parry, just found. He came in carrying a file, said, "Good evening," and seated himself at the cheap and nasty desk, his big, hard bulk dwarfing the little chair. Pete remained standing. "Well now, sir," the Super said, "quite a little job we've had to find you. We have a few questions to ask. Your name is Clifton Edward Parry?"

"Clifton Edward Parry." The man smiled. "That's right."

"And you live at—?"

"Ah. No fixed address, I expect you'd call it. Yes—no fixed address." The smile became a beam shared equally between the two policemen, as though the man felt they would be pleasured by his use of their own vernacular.

"You were—discovered—living in the city. Number 8 Fanthorpe Street. Suburb of Ellesdon."

"Sometimes. Sometimes."

"Sometimes?"

"Sometimes, I live there. It's a lodging house. I have several; I like to move about."

"And where have you moved to lately, sir? Since you came out of hospital?"

"Oh—London—Slough—Doncaster. Durham. Dumphries."

"All in a few weeks?"

"Yes. So many places to see, so many interests to look after." A sigh, a slow shaking of the fluffy head. "One will never cover them all."

He *is* bloody mad, Pete thought. London, yes. But he'd have to belt about like a trump in a collander. Billy the Fumer was speaking again.

"And this town? Have you been in this town? Say—last week?"

"Last week? I *may* have been. I go to so many places. Not that there's much in this town, is there?"

"Not unless you were interested in a Mr. and Mrs. Grover. Thomas Grover."

The man replied with a phrase straight out of an old-fashioned detective novel, his smile unwavering. "Don't play games with me, Inspector. Grover is dead. So is my bitch of a wife."

Policemen come up against many peculiar people. We've got a right one here, Pete thought. Thinks he's talking to Maigret.

96

"Dead, Mr. Parry?" the Super was saying, quite gently. "What makes you believe they are dead?"

"I killed them. Years ago."

"Years ago?"

"Years and years. At first they kept coming back, but not after I electrocuted them. *Zooph!* they went, just like that." The man snapped his fingers. "Sizzled to a cinder."

Ah well, said Pete's talking head, you can't win 'em all. And being batty doesn't mean he didn't do it. On the contrary. It just makes it harder to pin.

The Super, leaning his great body back with a sigh, almost overbalanced the little wooden chair. It teetered a second before his forward jerk landed the front legs on the bare floor with a little thump. "Well now, sir," he said, as gently as before. "I expect you can do with a cup of tea."

"And two ginger biscuits," said Mr. Parry.

"And two ginger biscuits. Mr. Parsons, if you will call a policeman in to keep Mr. Parry company, we will go and arrange it."

"By all means," Pete said. He left the room, went to the door leading into the general office, poked his head in and said, "Who's doing nothing?"

"I am," a policeman said. He was actually sharpening a match, to pick lingering canteen steaklette out from between his teeth.

"Come along then, my son. I've got a nice nutter for you to look after."

"Oo, bloody hell," said the policeman. "Why don't I keep my big mouth shut?"

Journeying over the ten yards or so of corridor between office and interview room, Pete delivered a briefing. "Just sit with him, sit at the desk. Don't shove him, but encourage him to talk. If he mentions Tom Grover or anything about the fire last Thursday, tip us the wink when we come back in."

"Right," the policeman said.

No need to say more, or to inquire of Billy the Fumer whether this course of action was what he intended. Competent policemen do not need detailed instruction every step of the way. Obviously, if a man is loopy enough to ramble in fields of fantasy, he is not going to lead you far along the straight and narrow. And nothing he says will stand up, in court or anywhere else. So Billy was arranging brief privacy without giving disturbance to the subject, for a little conference.

Sure enough, when they were outside in the corridor he said, "What do you think about that, then?"

"As a fruitcake," said Pete. "If he's not playing it up."

"Always so bloody difficult to tell," Billy the Fumer said. "If he's acting it, with his history he can pull it forever."

"And if he's not, we're buggered. If he's got Grover, unless he gives it to us straight, there's no way we can get it out of him."

"Quite. We can't lean on him, it only gets up their nose if they are barmy, they go barmier than ever." Policemen know as well as any psychiatrist the often physically violent reaction of the mentally sick to mental pressuring, and the reaction of malingerers with a history who know how they should react. "And if he *has* got Grover—if we keep him here and nobody else is out there to look after the bugger, he could be starving to death. Which might suit Chummy very well. Chuckle chuckle, sitting around here knowing we are short-and-curlied."

"Mm." Tricky. Very tricky. "So what are you going to do with him?"

"Let him go, is the best thing."

"Or put him back in the bin."

"That won't do Grover any good."

"If he's got Grover."

"Yes. Well, we can't whack that out of him with rubber truncheons. If we get him back into the bin and Grover's found tied up and dead sometime, we're well up the river."

"He may have killed him already."

"There's that, of course. If he's got him. Look—get on the blower to the Old Man, you'll find him at home. I said we'd ring.

Tell him I'm letting the bloke go under obbo, if he approves."
That shifted the can. "And arrange a tail. Pairs, round the clock.
If he's got Grover, he'll probably go and have a look at him."

"If he's not too loopy to remember he's got him. Or where he
left him."

"I'm not too sure," Billy the Fumer said, "that the bugger's
loopy at all."

So ten minutes later Mr. Parry left the station a free man,
walking briskly down towards the bus station. Pete saw him off
and waited long enough on the steps to satisfy himself that two
men standing in chat on the street corner had fallen in behind at
a discreet distance before he turned and went into his office,
where the telephone rang almost as he sat down at his desk.
"Yes?" he said.

"Call for you," said the instrument. "A Mr. Wood, asking for
you personally."

Charlie. Who should have known better than to keep ringing.
The policeman sighed. It had turned into a long day, and if Parry
led those two men to Tommy, now or during the night, it was
going to be a lot longer. "Put him through," he said; and after the
go-ahead-please: "Hallo, Charlie. Nothing to report." Nothing
high brass would fling an arm around his shoulder for, if he did.

"Pete," said Charlie's voice. "Listen—we just found Mario."

"Mario? Tommy's Mario?" Only one Mario around here, so the
odds were pretty good. "Found him?"

"Yes. Sally found him."

"What do you mean, found him?"

"You know the old sheep pen on the towpath—between Stipperton and Wenden Stavely? He was in there—still is—spark
out. Bump on his nog. I'm calling from Baker's Farm, just rang
for an ambulance. Thought I'd better give you a bell, he looks to
me as if he's concussed. Shock, you know. I didn't move him
because you never know."

"Hang about—what was Sal doing in a sheep pen?"

"Went in for a pee, you know how they are." After all, Pete

walked in the country with his own wife. "Know what I think, don't you? I think he was in that van—or waiting by the bridge, or something. No—he'd have been in the van, thrown clear or something—missed the explosion, anyway—got hit by something or got blown onto his head or something—staggered off along the towpath—had enough sense left to get under that shelter—that's where he was, under the shelter—and flaked out."

"Hold on, hold on." I'll tell you what you were doing, you and Sal, sneaking along by the river: You were making for the bridge, by the crafty route. Bypassing the lads keeping the rubbernecks away. That's naughty, in an ex-copper and a wife who writes for the paper. "Where's Sal now?"

"I left her with him. Listen—this is getting bloody funny. Does Tom fit into this? I mean—what was Mario doing in a van full of explosives?"

"Who said it was explosives?"

"Well—the telly, didn't it?"

That's right—it did. No way of sitting on that fact, the reporters would have worked it out for themselves, instanta. Charlie had not finished talking.

"They reckoned the driver was blown to bits. That wouldn't have been Tom, would it?"

"We've no reason to think so." Sod you—you're too pro. So is she, she'll be putting two and two together.

"Got reason for wondering, though, haven't you? Don't tell me we're the only ones with enough brain to link up Mario and Tommy and all the rest of it."

"We?"

"Me and Sally. I'd done it before I shot off for the ambulance. She'll have done it by now. And she's going to want the story. Can't blame her, can you? It can be a bloody great scoop; she's never had one before."

Pete spoke with considerable snap. "Don't let her do anything. It's delicate ground." He snapped for self-protection as much as anything. Special Branch was coming for this, could be arriving any minute. You never really knew if a switchboard is listening and leaking. If the Branch put on a clamp-down, he would not want it told that he had been in private discussion with a civvy friend whose wife phoned in the story and filed it under the very nose, nullifying the clamp before it went on. Her paper did not come out on Sunday, they'd have time to smother publication—but look at the leak-potential, from her office and from here. Bugger not about with Special Branch. And be seen by the switchboard, should it be ear-wigging, not to so bugger.

"Oh, come on, mate," Charlie was saying, "it doesn't take a lot of sorting out, does it? What were you doing on it, you and Billy? *And* the Old Man. All in glorious natural colour, poking about down there. You're on the Tommy job. And here's bloody Mario."

"It's down to Special Branch." Yes—there's bloody Mario. Where's this caper leading? Mario *and* Tommy, in that van?

"Is it, bechrist. Official Secrets Act? Ai ai—here comes the ambulance. Didn't hang about, did they? This 999 lark really works."

And it really does. By now, police in this very building would know of a man found unconscious in a sheep pen. But nobody would bother Pete with it, he was fully booked. "Where's the ambulance come from?"

"The hospital, I suppose; it's not one of ours." By ours, he meant police. Once a copper, always a copper. "Town, it'll be, they couldn't have got it out from the city in the time."

"You going down with him?"

"Well, yes. I suppose so." After all, they could hardly dust off the hands and abandon the poor lad.

"Hang about there, I'll be along. Soon as I've had a word with the Fumer. And tell Sal not to do anything until I've seen her."

"Right. Only don't bugger her about, she's a bit umpty as it is."

There were two hospitals in town, but one was maternity. Mario would not be taken there. It left only St. Thomas's, and

Detective Chief Inspector Parsons arrived there very soon after the ambulance did, with Charlie and Sally Wood driving along behind it. They came fast through the town, very fast; but no copper offered let or hindrance because they were obviously attached to the screaming vehicle and the squad car in front of that.

The policeman saw them as soon as he came through the swing doors, standing in the reception area with a lost look. He'd known they had arrived, their car was outside with the squad car and the ambulance, which stood with its back doors open. He said, "Hi, Charlie. Hallo, Sal. Where is he?"

Charlie indicated inner swing doors. "They took him through there."

"Let's go, then," said Pete, and led on; through the doors and along a short, bare and harrowingly scrubbed passage. The two policemen from the squad car stood outside a room. Pete nodded to them. "Evening, lads. In here, is he?"

"Evening, sir," one of the policemen said. "Quack's examining him; he says keep out."

"Does he? How quaint." And on, straight through the door.

They strip a man and whip him into bed in no time, at St. Thomas's. Mario was not quite in, he was lying on the bottom sheet with the top coverings not yet pulled up and tucked in, naked except for his underpants. He had the good, off-olive physique most often seen posing and throwing big coloured balls about on southern Italian beaches, unswollen as yet by pasta. A black nurse stood by with a white sister, and a youngish brown doctor bent over him. This doctor glanced up as they came in, irritation showing in his glossy black eyes. He said,

"Nobody to enter, plizz."

"Police, Doc," said Pete, flashing his little ID card. "Detective Chief Inspector Parsons."

The doctor looked down again, to carry on with his examination. Sally, obedient to nature in the midst of her concern, thought: You wouldn't think he was that beautiful, would you, to see him in his clothes? And look at that nurse, she's got her eye on him. They stood in silence until the doctor straightened, took his stethoscope out of his ears, pocketed the little thin-beamed light he had used to peer into Mario's eyes, and said in Pakistani near-Welsh:

"Nothing too serious, I think nothing broken. He's had a jolly good bang."

"How nice for him," said Pete. The nurse grinned widely, showing beautiful teeth.

"Concussed, quite badly. Blow on the temple, very fortunate. He will be all right."

"How soon can I talk to him?"

"Difficult to prophesy. He may be conscious in an hour, two hours. Maybe tomorrow. But he may not be fully compos mentis even then. A blow such as this upon the temple is not entirely conducive to clear thought." Up and down his voice went, very much like an impression of Peter Sellers.

"Right. Thanks. Sister—you'll be in charge of him? I'll leave a man to ring me as soon as he comes round. Can we get a cup of tea?"

"In the reception area," said Sister. "You'll find a machine on the wall."

"Good. I'll be there for the next ten minutes." Pete turned to lead the way back to reception.

Forty-five pence it cost to extract three paper cups of coffee from a machine offering that, or tea, or tomato soup. As so many visitors have said, plaintive or belligerent according to disposition: It's not so much the money, but do you call this bloody coffee? Girls who do duty at the reception desk curse the day that damn machine was hammered to the wall, the more aggressive punters appear to blame them for it. People seem to accept scummed-up and horrible tea, or the letter-box lurid sludge of soup, but they do get cross about the coffee.

Pete stood treat, inserting his money and bearing the three hot and handleless, squashy beakers over to where Sally and Charlie had seated themselves, with the easy skill of a man well used to transporting several pints across pubs after cricket. He sat down, facing them across a little low table set with back copies of *The Lancet* and *Nursing Mother,* and said, "Cheers." They took the first sip. He said, "God Almighty! Oh well. Now then—I can give you five minutes."

"Why can't I ring in my story?" Sally demanded.

"What's with Mario and Tom?" said Charlie.

Pete replied to Sally. "Because Billy the Fumer says no. Not yet."

"Billy the Fumer can't stop me, the law—"

"He can't stop you writing it, but he can stop Harry from publishing it."

"Why, for God's sake?"

"He's got to wait for an okay."

"Who from?"

Charlie put the answer in. "Special Branch."

"The Old Man."

"Let's not sod about," said Charlie. "The Old Man waits on Special Branch. Right? Why else is he sitting on it? It's straight news stuff. And the more you can splash about, the greater the chance of John Public spotting somebody they saw a picture of in the paper. Right? Like Tommy? If he didn't blow up with the truck."

"And if he did, which God forbid," said Sally, "somebody's going to get on to the story and Harry'll have my guts if I fell over it and keep it quiet."

"We're not talking about Tommy—"

"Course we bloody are," said Charlie. "It all ties in, doesn't it? Mario—thrown out, must have been, got conked—somebody went up with the truck—explosives. It's IRA or something. Isn't it? Terrorists—something."

"You're letting your imagination run away—"

"No—*you're* letting your imagination run away, mate. You've called in Special Branch. That means it's not straight CID stuff. Right?"

Pete hesitated a moment. Then he grinned, a bit lopsidedly. "My luck. To think I taught him how to do it. All right—I'll put you in the picture. But it's strictly off the record."

It took only a couple of minutes. About the only thing they did not already know was that the van belonged, according to the registration, to Tommy. And, of course, they had not heard of the picking up of Clifton Parry. He ended: "So there you are. We don't know if Tom's alive or dead, we don't know who he's mixed up with, we don't know what Mario's part of it is. We don't know if this Parry's a nutter or not, we don't know where the other geezer is, this Kelly geezer. We don't know who was in the van, or where it came from. The bloody plot keeps thickening, and we don't know nuffin."

"Julie," said Sally. "Oh—poor Julie—poor baby—"

"Poor Tom, if he knew who bombed 'em and why," said Charlie. "That'd be nice for him, wouldn't it, if he brought it on them all?"

"Well, there you have it." Pete speaking. "And, of course, we can't discount the fact that *he* might be after *them*. Or him— Parry or the Kelly geezer."

"It's a helluva story," Sally whispered. Shock, reawakened horror, and pressman's lust warred in her eyes.

"And you're not going to use it," said Pete, "are you? Not until I give the word. Know why? Because they'll hang me up by the you-know-what for telling you, and I'm a mate. Am I right? I trust you because we are friends, and friends of Tommy and Julie."

He'd hit it, he'd found the one sure way to hold the bar up. "Oh, you bastard," she said. "You wicked, evil bastard."

"I know." He grinned at her, with no great degree of happiness but freely now, knowing he was safe; took a sip at his coffee and

105

grimaced. "Holy God—what do they do, empty the specimen bottles into it? Anybody want another?"

"After that," said Charlie, "no."

Pete rose. "Well," he said, "I'll tell one of the boys inside to stay on as guard. Back to the sweat and tears. Write it up, Sal, and stand it by. Soon as it's released, I'll see you get a head start. And if anybody else comes sniffing at it before then, I'll be on to you."

"You'd better be. You bastard."

"See you, then," said Pete; and just before he moved away he had another thought. "Could even be something to do with the Mafia. Mario's Italian, they've got branches everywhere. Sweet Jesus, make it stop."

He left then; and when he got back to the station Billy the Fumer rang down to say that the lads tailing Parry had been on. They lost him in the city.

9

The inquest, put back already after the preliminary establishment of identities because of the disappearance of the next of kin, opened on Monday morning and was promptly adjourned, the police requesting it until they had completed further investigation that could well have major influence on the verdict. There was no doubt that a person or persons unknown had unlawfully killed them, and probably with intent. But probability is not sufficient in law to move the finding up from manslaughter to murder. Back went the pitiful bodies to the ultimate indignity of a tray in the deep freezer.

Charlie and Sally were there, but as friends only. Neither was engaged professionally—the story was covered, of course, by a solid body of the press, among them young Arnie Poddle from her own paper, and Charlie, by reason of his firm's having to argue any insurance claim, must later inspect and report on the van, transferred by now to the police pound—but their presence was in the name of friendship. Somebody must be there, if only to soften the terrible inhumanity of it for Julie's parents, come down from Chester. Pete Parsons attended with Billy the Fumer, who applied for the adjournment; and Tony Scully was there, ready to present the Fire Brigade conclusions. And, of course, there were the parents.

Nice people, they were, dressed in fitting black. Not really so small, but looking shrunken, as people do in the half-stunned condition of shock and racking grief. They emerged from the courtroom to stand as if bewildered on the steps, flanked by the bulk of Superintendent Fumery and the not much lesser solidity of Pete Parsons. Taken together, this muscular beef would make infinitely more robust characters appear fragile.

Charlie and Sally went across to introduce themselves. Said they were friends, lived next door; expressed condolences very obviously sincere, since Sally's eyes were brimming and she needed her handkerchief to dab away tears spilling over. There were no tears from the parents, and little attempt at conversation. Their weeping, perhaps, was all done, and they could hardly be expected to chatter away like happy green budgies.

The little they did say was spoken quietly, without interest. Yes, they came down last night. By the late train. No, they would not be staying (Sally asked with the guest room in mind; better for them than a hotel), they would go back now. There was a train at eleven-fifteen.

"We'll run you to the station," Sally said on impulse, needing to offer something of herself. They had no car there.

"That's all arranged," said Superintendent Fumery, with weight. "Chief Inspector Parsons is seeing to it."

She might have known that, would have, no doubt, at a less emotional time. She said, "Ah. Of course."

Pete Parsons spoke. Perhaps he felt that having them along would help to spread his own load, especially during that time, difficult to bridge even among unstressed friends, between arrival at a station and departure of the train. "You can come along, if you wish." He glanced at his guv'nor, who nodded. It was not, after all, an official journey.

At twelve minutes past eleven they stood on the sunny platform. But for the black-clad parents, the two men would have discarded their sober jackets long ago, and Sally was sweating under her two-piece suit. Conversation was very sparse. Nobody had thought it would not be. Julie's mother said, just before the train arrived,

"To think they shouldn't have been there at all, they should have been with us."

The men let Sally answer. "How do you mean?"

"Julie and the baby—they should have arrived in the afternoon. For a visit. But Father had one of his turns, so I rang her and she said they'd drive up in the morning."

"Tommy, too?"

"No. Well—maybe later. He doesn't always—didn't always—come with them."

"Sometimes," the father said, "he'd come up in a day or two. Sometimes he wouldn't. Depended on business."

"It doesn't matter so much nowadays," said the mother. "Does it, with everybody driving about in their own cars? I never have got used to her driving."

The train was running into the station. Pete asked, "Were they coming for any particular reason?"

"No," said the lady. "Julie rang a few days before and said they'd be up for a visit." Inconsequentially, she added, "The country is very nice around Chester." And further conversation was rendered impossible by the grinding squeal of brakes, the general business of boarding and farewell.

Sally waved. Pete and Charlie raised a saluting hand each. The train squealed again as it drew out. They went back through a morose and crumbling ticket hall where, amid old orange peel, fag-ends, abandoned luggage trolleys, and a vandalised telephone booth, a glum character peered through a grimy ticket window set between posters saying THIS IS THE AGE OF THE TRAIN, and slammed themselves into Pete's car, left on the forecourt. As they drove off, Sally said,

"Julie didn't mention that they were going away. I was talking to her in the afternoon. So were you, Charlie, weren't you, when you were in the garden?"

"Yes." Warm and smiling she was, curved and creamy in her tiny bikini. "If I were Tom tonight . . ." he'd said to himself.

"You'd have thought Tommy would have said something, wouldn't you?"

All three had investigative training. All three had honed aptitude. All three were thinking: Was he getting them away? Because he feared something might happen? Did he fail to mention afterwards—it is the sort of thing the bereaved tongue seizes on, as Julie's mother's had—that they should not have been there because he knew the something had happened, and he was involved in bringing it about? Did Julie, even, *know* why she was going? Or at least, know she was being sent clear for some bent reason?

But none of them put it into words. Instead, Charlie asked, "What about Tom? Are you still working on this Parry geezer?"

"They bloody lost him."

"Who did?"

"The two half-wits on tail. Back to bloody uniform for them."

"Oh, nicely, nicely. So you're no nearer? How'd they come to do that?"

"Not entirely their fault, I suppose, but Billy's chopping 'em. They got on the fast bus behind him. It stops outside C and A's, in the Wheatrow. He got off and went straight in, and they were held up by some fat old bird slipping on the stairs. Flat on her back. Time they got over her he'd vanished. Once you lose 'em in a store like that it's a sod of a job to pick 'em up again. Escalators—stairs—lifts. And if he knew they were about, he'd be in, straight through, out the back door, and thank you kindly."

"Have you got his drum staked?"

"We've got everywhere staked," Pete snapped. "The bastard's got lost."

Neither Sally nor Charlie said, as they might have done: cockup. Pete clearly was disturbed by the happening. Nothing but a falling-out to be gained by pressing. Charlie said instead,

"Anything on anything else?"

"Nothing. And Mario's still out."

"He must have taken a helluva whack. Or the blast hit him."

"Grrmmph," said Pete; and they were silent until they reached the town centre, where he put them off. Charlie's car was still in

110

the courtyard car park, ready to take him to the city, and work. He said to Sally,

"What time you due at the office?"

"Any time, really," she said. "I've got nothing in the book until this afternoon."

"Coffee?"

"Why not?"

"We could go to the Belle Epoque. You might get an angle from Hans. Let's have this bloody jacket off."

The Belle Epoque was, in fact, starting from the courthouse, about the nearest place for a cup of coffee, certainly for a good one. A left turn, a right turn, and *voilá*—open from 11 A.M. But this morning, when they reached there, it was not open.

"That's funny," Sally said. "Where's Hans?" Nothing odd about no French chefs, they arrived later for the lunchtime trade. But Hans was German, and a German who has a set time of arrival and a duty to be there will arrive—this one never missed—on time. The door opened at eleven o'clock, to the very minute.

"Do you think the police have pulled him? Mixed up in it?"

"Pete didn't say so."

"Pete didn't say much at all."

"Well—it's a bit early to worry, isn't it?" Sally checked her watch. "He's only half an hour late."

"That's a lifetime, for Hans. Of course, he may be sick. Or on a driving job. But I think I'll give Pete a buzz, just in case."

"Just in case of what?"

"Just in case I don't, and the bugger's vanished. Get up Pete's nose, that would. End of private confidences. There's a booth in Charlotte Square."

Pete took the call almost as he entered the station. He rang Mr. Phillips, at the haulage depot. No, said Mr. Phillips, Hans was not down for a driving job today. He hadn't been in, wasn't there now. So Pete rang through to Superintendent Fumery,

111

closeted in his office with Special Branch men. Better go down, said Billy, have a look. And you'll need somebody to check on his home address, of course?

Pete sorted out Hans' home address—not difficult, if subject is an alien—and radioed for the beat patrol car to call there. He then went to the Belle Epoque, where the French chefs had arrived by now and were standing about outside, wondering how to get in. No sign of Charlie and Sally. This did not surprise him, he'd told Charlie on the phone there was no need for them to hang about. Used a tone of voice saying he'd sooner they didn't. Yes, he'd said—he'd see that Sally got the story—*if* there was a story to get.

One reason for wanting them out of the way: Normally, policemen do not advertise the bunch of assorted keys they carry. By the book, to use them constitutes illegal entry. Nevertheless, Pete produced his now to unlock the door, discounting the French chefs. After all, their friend and colleague might have collapsed in there, or something. But nobody was about, no coffee bubbling. Even the morning paper lay undisturbed on the mat.

He emerged to find the car radio squawking. The beat men, speaking from Hans' digs. Hadn't been seen since he left for work on Saturday. Nobody reported it; Saturday was his late night, the landlady was invariably asleep when he came in, and he often spent the whole of the weekend away, or shut up alone in his room. He cooked for himself. She led an active Bingo and Olde-Tyme Dancing Life, so sometimes she did not see him from rent day to rent day.

He radioed to the station, asking for a guard to be sent down. Then he went back into the restaurant to fetch out the chefs, who seemed bewildered by the whole proceeding. "You'd better go home," he said. "Just let me have your addresses, we'll contact you as soon as we sort things out." And he relocked the door. Couldn't leave them to open up and do the best they could; somebody might want to dust the place all over for fingerprints, Forensic might need to sift flour dust and peer at cigarette ends.

"Meestair Mario weel not be glad," the leading chef said, "eef we not here when he come."

"Don't worry about a thing," Pete told him. "Just go home, put your feet up, and read the paper. Leave everything to us."

"He weel not laike for lose business, for lose monais—"

"Nobody likes for lose monais. Good morning."

They walked away, volleying French at each other. Pete waited until his guardian constable arrived before he got into his car and drove away, thinking, Another bloody complication. Gone missing? Scarpered? Fell foul of—Mario?—and Tommy?— Got himself done?

Or gone up with the truck? In which case, it wasn't Tommy. Tommy was still a missing person.

Unless: There is room to seat three in the cab of a Dodge van, using the padded central engine cover. Some actually have three seats. The police ones had, in the days when the police used Dodges.

So: Did *two* men blow to smithereens?

Bloody hell.

"The fact of the matter is, gentlemen," said the Chief Constable, "it's all rather complicated." He was speaking in his well-panelled office, seated at the beautiful desk. Detective Chief Superintendent Fumery and Detective Chief Inspector Parsons sat on the guest chairs. The Superintendent said,

"It is that, sir."

"Special Branch is taking over the IRA angle or whatever, so that hardly concerns us. They appear, as we know, to link it up with the dump robbery at Bovey Tracey a year ago. Which ties them in with us, since our missing man Grover appears to own the van. So now we have people missing who may be alive or may be dead, a fire killing two people that *may* have to do with the Irish or other terrorists, or *may* have to do with one or other of two men known to utter threats against our missing Grover, one of whom we cannot find and the other of whom we let go and lost. We have a man under guard in hospital whom we cannot interview because he is unconscious, and a *possible* protection gang of whom there is no trace, but who *may* have started the fire. Would you say that fairly sums up the position?"

"Yes, sir," said Billy the Fumer. "Mm. That's about it."

Put like that, Pete thought, it sounds like a sticky little problem.

"Mm." The Chief Constable was not looking particularly content. "Uh-huh. Well, this far, we appear to have no reason for expecting Home Office commendation."

Billy the Fumer's reply had a good deal of snap in it. He was beginning to fume again, and when he fumed not even the high and mighty were sacrosanct. "Early days yet, sir; the case isn't even off the floor."

"Early days," the Chief said. "Mm. One wonders how we will cope if it does get off the floor. You say you obtained ingress to the restaurant, Mr. Parsons?"

"Yes, sir." Forensic was there by now, with powder and soft brushes.

"May one ask how you managed it?"

Oh no, Pete thought, you don't catch me with that one. Open secret, the detective's unofficial little bunch, winked at roguishly because very, very often it is so useful. But the Chief in his present mood was pushing at it. "One of the chefs had a key, sir," he said smoothly.

The Chief let it pass over. He'd carried a bunch himself in his day. Start not in moodiness a rabbit you may regret later, having committed yourself to chasing it right into a hole in the ground. He veered away, saying,

"Well, gentlemen, it seems all we can do is carry on beavering. Live in hope. A six-foot-three German we may conceivably trace—"

"Unless he's shot out of the country," Mr. Fumery snapped.

"In which case we must rest our faith in Interpol. All right, gentlemen, thank you. Unless somebody has a better idea, that will be a—" The intercom telephone buzzed. He picked it up. "Yes? Yes. Uh-huh. Right." He flicked the little cutout switch. "Well," he said, "that's something. Your man in the hospital is awake."

When they had seen Mario, the brown doctor conducted the two policemen along the corridor to the Medical Superintendent's office, talking all the way. He used his fluid hands to invite use of the chairs provided and himself perched on the edge of the desk, talking still.

". . . The brain, you see, is a very funny thing; there are no hard-and-fast rules. As I say, X-ray showed a slight fracture not apparent upon my preliminary examination, causing some compression. Concussion followed by compression—"

Superintendent Fumery, seating himself, cut in. "What it amounts to, Doctor, is that now he's awake, we can't get anything out of him. Right?"

"As I was saying," the doctor said, "concussion followed by compression leads quite commonly to loss of memory—"

"How long for?"

"Quite impossible to say."

"A day? A week? A month?"

"It could be any of these. Or longer."

"Longer?"

"If it causes permanent damage, the condition may persist for life."

"Marvellous!" the Superintendent exploded. "Bloody marvellous!" He fixed the medical man with a baleful eye, as if it were all his fault.

Chief Inspector Pete Parsons spoke. "What I don't understand is how he could make his way right along the towpath to that sheep pen, if he was unconscious."

"Surprising, is it not?" The doctor turned to him eagerly, an enthusiast seizing happily upon the one of two laymen capable of showing intelligent interest in the mysteries of his own absorbing

115

speciality. "But by no means unique. There was the famous case in Newcastle, the pregnant young lady knocked down by a car. Got up and went home, carried on for two days quite normally before she collapsed. Unconscious from when the car hit her for nine months, they kept her on ice. Baby delivered in the normal way, when she came to she never remembered a thing about it. Mind of a child, they even had to teach her her ABC—".

"You mean we have to teach him his ABC before we can talk to him?" said Billy the Fumer. "In a year's time?"

"One cannot make any prognostication," the doctor said. "The brain is a most funny thing. One is glad to say, she is now living happily with the child and her husband. Full recovery. But, of course, she remembers nothing of her life before she awoke to find herself a mother. Which would appear to indicate that the pains of childbed are largely psychosomatically induced. Of course one cannot wax dogmatic upon so complex a thesis, but Bomsplitz says in his book here—"

Billy the Fumer rose to his feet. Pete Parsons had no need to, having not sat down. "Thank you, Doctor. We will see you again, no doubt. I'll leave my man here, to notify me at once of any change."

By the sound of it, Pete thought, he could be sitting there until his pension is due. The doctor was saying, as he withdrew the slim brown hand reaching for a tome: "Ah. Yes. My pleasure. Good day."

"Good day," said the policemen.

They made their way out from the hospital, leaving the doctor to nip off for a quick cup of tea and Mario lying with open eyes frowning into space under the turban of his bandages. No remembrance in him of restaurant, or panic, or van, or blast, or of the chunk of bridge parapet that flew high in the air and came down *wump* on his head. Good job it was not a main chunk, one of those would have crushed his skull flat to the jawbone.

Sally was at the office when the boy came round dropping a copy of the paper on each desk, as he did every day before it went onto the street. She put aside her pencil—first drafted notes for her column she did always in pencil—and picked it up. The great banner headline screamed: SLAUGHTER AT WENDEN STAVELY; and that was all right. But the sub-heading asked: IRA INVOLVED? Her heart suddenly leaping, she read on; and as she did so, anger grew in her. She had been betrayed.

The national dailies had featured the story, of course, but without mentioning specific details—no mention of IRA, or any hint of terrorist involvement. Presumably the Special Branch in London, or the Metropolitan Police Anti-Terrorist Squad, had sat upon editorial speculation. Nor did they mention, because they did not know, that the town police believed the van might have been driven by the missing man Thomas Grover, and that he was missing now in the completest possible way.

But here was her story, the one she told Harry must not, *must not* be used until release came from the police—who would ring her, she had said, in the person of Pete Parsons, so that they would leap into action a mile ahead of *everybody*. Dailies—provincials—*everybody*.

It spread from the front page to cover the whole of pages two and three, combining the story filed in the routine way by the lad sent to the scene with her own. There were outline details of the crash, there was mention of the fact that the van had exploded, there was full weight given, naturally, since they lived within the paper's circulation area, to the dead lads—all of this from the reporter's story. But he had said nothing about IRA or even explosives, and nothing about Tommy. She knew it, she had read his copy. He had delivered the official line: The police are attempting to trace the driver of the van, who is believed to have died in the crash.

All this naming Tommy as owner and possible driver, all this about police believing the van to have been carrying explosives for use by the IRA, the bit about Mario and a possible Mafia tie-up—this was hers. Harry had scooped the pool, all right. The agencies would be on to this, the nationals would be down like carrion crows.

She got up from her desk and made her furious way to the editor's private office, bursting in through the door to fling the paper on his desk. "What's this?" she demanded.

He raised pouched eyes from his never-ending task of marking up copy, a bald and big-chinned, weary-looking man with a blue pencil in his hand. Harry Vincent worked here man and boy forty years. "I like people to knock before they come in," he said.

"Never mind that. What about this?"

"What about it?" Nothing defensive marking him, nothing of guilt or unease. He sat in his shirt sleeves, and if there was sweat on his forehead—well, it was hot in here. There was sweat under his arms, too, you could tell by the stains on his shirt.

"It was supposed to be held, pending police release. There's a bar on it—"

"I haven't heard of any bar."

"You bloody well have—I told you about it."

"Officially, I haven't heard of any bar."

"Did you check with Pete Parsons?"

He snapped his fingers. "I knew there was something. Slipped my mind."

Too angry to realize that he was needling her, she said, "You know what it means, don't you? You've breached the Official Secrets Act. You can go to gaol for it."

She was a good girl. Good writer, too, probably had a future. But she was young. Enjoyable, to needle the young. Kept them on their toes. He had, in fact, checked, not with Pete, but with the Press Officer at the station. The bar imposed by the Chief Constable in deference to Special Branch they had waved aside when they arrived. But why tell her? *You're* in breach of the Official Secrets Act, sweetie," he said. "Not me, I just printed your story in good faith."

"Good faith?" she blazed. "That's bloody funny—I told you—"

"Never rely on verbals. You should know that. Put it down in writing. Three copies, and get one signed."

"You bastard."

No outward sign that he was enjoying himself. All this, on top of elation proper to the pressman who in his minor paper has just printed a beautiful scoop. "Why don't you come to tea some time?" he said. "I'd like to introduce you to Mother."

"Perhaps I'd better see my solicitor."

"In your own time, darling, not during working hours. I've seen mine already." Of course he had—the paper's legal advisors had made the actual call to the police. Lunatic, to plough on without making sure you are covered.

Sally, in fact, even in the midst of her raging uproar, knew this. But she needed something to hit him with. Confidences had been made to her as a friend, by a friend, with the command that it go no further. Apart from the harm premature revelation might do to the friend, apart from any kick-back it might bring to her, it affected Charlie. Pete was first and foremost Charlie's friend. And this was not some little clanger dropped, it was too big for anybody to sweep under the mat.

"The bar was put on by Pete Parsons," she snapped. "A friend. I suppose friendship and trust don't mean a damn thing to you."

"If you're staying in this business," said the editor, "you might as well learn that you can't trust anybody. And Pete Parson's a policeman. Right?"

"So?"

"Policemen and pressmen don't have any friends. Now bugger off, I'm busy."

The paper was on the street by the time Pete Parsons set out with Billy the Fumer to collect the known firebug Melvyn Kelly. Seedy men in cloth caps stood with bundles on little trestle tables at the corners in the town centre where they always stood. Each stall carried a placard, and the first one to catch Pete's eye yelled: EXPLODING VAN. IRA INVOLVED?

It was Billy the Fumer who stopped the car, saying, "Got any small change? Might as well see what they're up to."

The newspaper seller was no stranger, to Pete or to porridge. He said, "Hallo, Mr. Parsons. Hot, annit?"

"Keeping out of trouble, Albert?" said Pete. "That's a good boy." He nodded to the papers. "Give us one."

The vendor grinned like a dog, making his dog-like little joke. "Ain't giving 'em away, Guv. I'll sell you one."

Pete handed over his money, received the paper, and walked away. The newspaper seller relaxed slightly. He'd been afraid the bastard had come to discuss the matter of a quantity of lead stripped from a church roof and lying in his son's cellar.

Billy the Fumer let in the clutch, easing the car on its way. "You can read it to me," he said. "Pass the journey nicely, won't it?" Once again—it was never otherwise—with definite action to occupy him, the fret had passed away and joviality was restored.

"There's a helluva lot of it," Pete told him. "First three pages."

"Good. Good. It's quite a long way to Coventry."

Pete began to read aloud, and while he did so the unease that stabbed him when he saw the placard spread into anger. Careful not to let it colour his voice, he read unemotionally to the bottom of page 3. A certain gravity settled on Billy the Fumer as he listened. He said when Pete folded the paper,

"Mm. Mmm. Our Harry's had himself a field day. Scooped the lot, hasn't he? Nice change from flower shows and golden weddings." A time of silence, another half-mile eaten of the road to Coventry. "Leak somewhere, would you say?"

"There's no bar up," Pete said. "Special Branch took it off."

A police superintendent is no fool, and long years of dealing with urgent calls from editors seeking clarification or information to meet deadlines teaches him willy-nilly the facts of newspaper life. "That was later," he said. "He'd have needed to be set up before that. So he had all this while the Old Man's stop was still on. Didn't he?"

"Mm," said Pete. "I suppose he did. Although, of course, it doesn't take all that long to set up."

"Takes a bloody long time to write it, though, three pages of it. I think we'll have to take a look at this."

The cow, Pete was thinking. Serve me right—should never have told them *anything*. But—friends—Charlie and Sally—they of all people should know— If you can't trust friends aware of the form, whom can you bloody well trust?

Billy the Fumer was not bothered at all about the actual content of the printed story. When there is no block imposed, the police normally welcome the widest possible media coverage, for obvious reasons. Nor was he obsessively concerned about a leak; no bureaucratic body is watertight. But when a discernible can takes to the air, that man is wise who looks into the matter, to ensure that it settles on some other shoulder. So he would look into it. For now, he moved his mind back to the job in hand.

"I'm not sure we haven't made a mistake, having this Kelly character hauled in. I'm not sure we shouldn't have said from the start: Leave 'em alone, just put a tail on." It had been a blunder, pulling in the man Parry and losing him, alerted now to police interest.

"You could be right," said Pete.

"Well, it's too late now. We've got him. Let's just hope he leads us to your friend Grover. If there's any Grover left to be led to."

And to tell the truth, the junior man thought, I doubt if there is by this time, even if he was not the one who went up with the van.

"Trouble is," said Billy the Fumer, "it's all happened in the wrong order. If we'd known about the Special Branch angle before your man was listed as missing, I'd have approached differently. And if he *did* blow up with the gear, we're wasting our bloody time on this Coventry trip." He drove on for a while. Then he said, "Problem is, we don't know, do we? Is he skiting about with the angels, or has one of these buggers got him stashed somewhere? We don't know, do we? Tell you what—if he blew up we'll have a helluva job pinning anything on anybody, without an identifiable body."

The man Kelly had been picked up by the Coventry police, shopped by a little man in return for the favour of a whisper in the judge's ear. Many, many wanted men are landed that way. This one had been carrying on with his normal life in the city, secure behind a beard and moustache and National Health spectacles, all donned since he came out of prison. In no way did he tally up to the old official photographs in the police file, two profiles and a full-face with number underneath. Unfortunately, the normal life of the bent gravitates by natural law to shoulder-rubbing with the bent. The underworld in Coventry knew who he was. A little man shopped him. Simple as that.

Billy had decided not to bring him back to the town. No sense in it. If he did have Tommy, he would not have stowed him there. Most likely he would be here, as live soul or as cadaver. Coventry, agreed, is not on the route between the town and Chester; but in the day of the motor car, what does that matter? In you get with a gun on the driver, and tell him to drive you anywhere.

So they saw him in an interview room at the great city force headquarters, where no boards creak underfoot, no old dried-up galoshes are found in cupboards papered over fifty years ago, and there are no mice.

The interview was not a long one. Billy was regretting the fact that he was conducting it. Given his time over, he would have moderated that EMTAD call. Tails on, and nobody alerted. If Grover was still alive, unobtrusive round-the-clock surveillance would probably have led straight to him. Somebody had to visit the place where he was being held some time.

And this man was a very different proposition from Parry. This one was a professional, and nimble-witted. He sat in the interview room as though he belonged there, entirely at ease. A small-ish man, bald but with this thick, dark growth covering jaws and upper lip. With his head on upside down, he'd have had a fine stand of hair.

Yes, he'd known Grover. No, he hadn't seen him, not for years. Yes, he knew he was missing, he read the papers, didn't he, he watched TV. No, he hadn't known the police wanted to see him. Why ask him about it?

The Superintendent did not press the fact that the man had vowed vengeance at the time of his gaoling, and all through his stretch in prison. No profit in working him over; the more he was chivvied, the less he would say. He might even enjoy it—he looked as though he was inviting it even now, grinning through his whiskers and his National Health horn-rims. Not very attractive, the National Health spectacle frames; but then, it would have taken more than tailor-made eye-furniture to make this one lovely. So Billy merely said,

"We are interviewing everybody who knew him, sir." Impassive. Not so much as a hint of satiric emphasis on the "sir." But not convincing. Not to a pro. "And you seem to have known him rather well."

"Oh, I knew him all right," said Kelly. "I knew him, you may believe me. I'll tell you something else you already know: I'd have killed the bastard gladly."

Pete put his word in. "Past tense, Mr. Kelly?"

"Past tense, Mr. What's-Name."

"You think he's dead?"

"I think he's dead. And I may be wrong. And I'll tell you what you think. You think you've cocked it up." Teeth were glimmering through the whiskers. And not bad teeth; they, too, were National Health. The teeth are marginally better than the spectacles. The grin was widening, the eyes sparkling behind the lenses, crinkled with pure malice. He was smart, all right; he was all the way down to the nub of it. "Because if you've pulled everybody who hated him enough to do it, if one of us *has* got him we're not going back to him now, are we? Not with you putting a tail on and all. Let's say I've got him. Haven't killed him because before he dies I want him to suffer. Well—now I walk away, don't I? I don't go near anymore, I get my kick out of knowing he's dying because he's not being fed and watered, and watching you lot blunder about, all cocked up."

"Very interesting train of thought," said Superintendent Fumery. His wattles were red.

"Don't tell me you hadn't got that far." The grin became an outright chuckle. "Beautiful, really, isn't it? From any point of view, looks as though he's had it. Marvellous. I hope the bastard died in agony. No—I hope he's still doing it. Good luck to whoever's got him. And now, if that's all, I'll be on my way. You have my address; let me know when you find him."

"You'll go," Fumery retorted, "when I say you can go." Another mistake, brought on by a frustrated wish to smash those gleaming choppers down the man's throat.

"Wrong. You've got nothing to charge me with; you can't hold me."

"We can keep you here, to assist in our inquiries."

"Do. A night or two's free board and lodging—very acceptable. Your breakfasts are rather good, usually. And where will it have got you? If I have Grover, he'll be dead, probably, before you turn me loose. You've cocked it up, Mr.— what did you say your name is? Haven't you?"

He was right. There was no crime, no misdemeanour even, with which they could charge him. Not even with obstructing the police—his presence here alone would stand, in a court of law, as evidence of his being willing to cooperate. Certainly, they'd had to fetch him; but he came readily enough, and not every citizen sought by the police knows that he is wanted. A good solicitor, in a case like this, can make the police look a right bunch of ham-fisted Percies. And to hold him might kill Grover. Somebody would have to answer to that, in view of the fact that he had been sought and brought in specifically to save Grover. But a policeman does not relish, anymore than does any man, being openly mocked by a slippery enemy. So Fumery said,

"Off the record, son. You're bent, and you're going to slip. You're going to slip because every minute from now on we'll be poking to make sure you do. And when you do—God help you."

"Threats, Mr. Thing?" the man said. "If I *had* got him, you wouldn't be doing him any favours."

"Get out," said Billy the Fumer. "Get out of my sight."

"Out of your sight?" The man Kelly got up from the nasty little wooden chair upon which he fitted so well, and he was still smiling. Gloating, but without cackling and rubbing his hands. "Surely not. What about the tail you'll put on me?"

When he was gone, Pete Parsons said, "Kelly is an Irish name."

"If you're thinking him into the Special Branch caper, forget it. Doesn't know a thing about it."

Pete had not really believed he did. The only paper to have blazoned the story did not circulate in Coventry. His mind, working in many directions at once, had simply connected the name with the Irish part of his thinking.

"Even so," said Superintendent Fumery, "we'll see if the Special Branch lads'd like to check him out. I'll nail the bastard one way or other, stake me on it."

Not so easy, though, thought Pete, with him in Coventry and you many miles away. But say nothing. And you might work it, there are wheels within wheels. Didn't even get the last word, did we? A most peculiar situation. And I'm glad you're in charge and not me, because there's no book to go by. There's no precedent.

Sally had gone back to the Belle Epoque during the afternoon, not to eat but to see what, if anything, was happening. She found it locked still, with a uniform policeman guarding the door. So something was definitely wrong. She said to the policeman, "What's up?"

"Don't ask me, miss," he said. "I'm just the doorman."

"Press," she said. *"Evening Courier."* She was clicking her handbag open, fetching out her pass.

"I know. If you want information, better ring the station." The police inevitably get to know the working press people in any town. This one did not intend to be quoted as the police spokesman who said today . . .

She turned away to walk back to the office. Not far, the business area is closely grouped round the town centre. This should be reported, written up as further development of the story; but to hell with it, Harry had landed her in deep enough already. Let him find out about it for himself, he'd get no more out of her. Whatever was in it, there'd be no inside tip from Pete. Not now.

She did ring the station later, before leaving for home. Not seeking information, but because the whole situation worried her. She had been expecting that Pete would call, if only to castigate her. But when no call came, her mind told her that he was finished with her, and with Charlie too, no doubt. He had withdrawn himself in contempt and anger. Worried, too, he'd be—he could hardly get out from under, if a breach in security was under scrutiny.

And it wasn't his fault. It wasn't her fault—Harry did it, the bastard. It wouldn't do Pete much good—he probably wouldn't speak to her anyway—but she must try to explain.

So she rang, and the station told her that Chief Inspector Parsons was out. She asked if they could tell her where he'd gone. Knowing very well but playing cagy—they'd have seen the paper by now—they said on official business. She hung up; and with no way of knowing he was in Coventry, she thought, he's dodging me. He's probably in his office. Tell her I'm out.

Of course, he may be out. But even if he is, he'd surely have rung, to tear me into strips.

She left the office; and for the first time since she joined the paper, walked past the editor's room without calling a cheery good night. Harry didn't notice. Head bent, he worked on, impervious to her virulent witch-wish crackling around him: that the police would shove, and shove him right up in front of the Press Council. Or worse, with no limit.

Oh, and the day went from bad to worse. Charlie arrived home before she had time even to make the cup of soothing tea normally efficacious at the start of her period when taken with a chocolate biscuit and two Paracetamol tablets. She needed sympathy, even, perhaps—women are equal now in all but this: their right to weep, and half fare on the bus at sixty—to splash a tear onto a shoulder still in fair, though used, condition; but he came in carrying the paper, which he flung down onto the kitchen table snapping, without kiss or how-are-you:

"What the hell is this?"

She fired defensively, at once. "What's what?"

"You know bloody well what. This. What about your promise to Pete?"

"I kept my promise to Pete."

"Like buggery. It's all here. All of it. He put the bloody bar up—"

"There was no bloody bar—Harry checked—"

"For you there was a bar. *He* put it up. Did you ring him, did he take it down?"

"He—"

"He didn't, did he? He didn't say anything to me when I rang—and this was set up before that. You know what you've done, don't you?"

"I didn't—"

"You've landed him in it. And yourself—and your bloody paper. *And* me. Us. So far as Pete's concerned, we're dead."

There are tears of remorse, tears of grief, tears of anger, tears stemming from sheer emotional over-tension. They were all in Sally, rising and threatening to burst their way out; but she stormed: "Don't shout at me! Don't you shout at me!" *Never* let 'em grind you down.

"Shout at you?" he shouted. "I ought to thump you, that's what I ought to do."

"Who the hell do you think you are?" she hooted.

"Who do I think I am? I'll tell you who I think I am—I'm a poor bastard married to a treacherous bitch who just sold him and his mate up the river for the sake of a bloody byline. That's who I am."

In fact, she did not even get a byline. Normally she would have had a go at Harry for that; the story was more than worthy and her name was known in the town. But this was not a normal story. She had noticed the absence, and actually felt relief. Who wanted to be named on this one?

"It isn't like that at all!" she cried loudly.

"No? What is it like, then?" Equally loud. At least.

And now the tears welled over. "It's Harry—Harry did it." She wailed it like a small girl desperate to evade retribution for something her brother has done, her face puckering as the sobs overwhelmed her.

The most liberated of men cannot face unflinching the sudden bursting into tears of the female in distress. "Oh, bloody hell," said Charlie. "Oh, for Christ's sake. Come on, now. Oh, bloody hell."

10

It was late when Pete Parsons and Billy the Fumer finished work last night, and early when they started again this morning. Nothing unusual about that, for CID men. After they got back from Coventry there was a conference with the two Special Branch men and the Chief Constable in that man's office.

There is no doubt about it, Special Branch and the Anti-Terrorist Squads work at their trade. These two had charts to show streets and even houses all over the area for a hundred miles around, each blue circle enclosing a point where suspected or proven sympathizers with various causes were known to live and/or foregather. They had files containing pictures of these people—and they were not all men—together with detailed accounts of their habits and behaviour patterns and lists of all the people with whom they were known to associate. The local men did not need telling, and the Special Branch men did not think it worthy of mention that these were merely the documents they had brought with them as most likely to be useful on this particular job. In London would be similar files covering the entire country. If you count in liaison with foreign agencies, the network covers almost the entire Western world. And still the terrorists slip through. Inevitably, since disguise is easy and there is always another, unknown as yet, to take the place of the captured and locked away.

In this particular case, none of the computerized documentation backed by a hot line to London was helping very much. Nothing was left of the explosive that went up with the truck, not so much as a morsel to be analysed in the hope that it might tell where it came from, Bovey Tracey as first favourite. And nothing was left but a few scattered shreds of the driver who, if he was Thomas Grover, did not feature on their lists anyway. All they knew of him was from prison records, studied to give them something to do.

The fact was, like the regular police, they were stymied. Temporarily, they hoped, because all those people in all the streets and houses ringed were now under twenty-four-hour surveillance. Something might come of it; but more, they felt, would come from Mario, if and when they could get at him. Give it a day or two, the man in London said. If there's no joy, you might as well come back. So they waited, two untidy men called Fowler and Figge. Wonderful names for a comedy act. But these were no comedians. They had jaws like man-eating pike and were very sparing with the smiles.

They were interested in Melvyn Kelly, who should have been Irish, surely, with a name like that. When Superintendent Fumery spoke of him—what about that for a comedy act? Fumery, Fowler, and Figge—they brought out the lists. Coventry rated a ring or two, and they had several Kellys; but these were scattered, never a one known ever to visit the city.

"Not that that means anything," said Fowler, who worked in scruffy, off-the-peg suiting but was nevertheless a superintendent. "They switch names like they change their socks. If they ever change their socks. He's worth pencilling in. What do you think, Harry?"

"Firebug—porridge merchant—shove him down," said Figge. An inspector, with jeans, desert boots, a sweatshirt, and no discernible respect for rank. "We'll see what London's got on him. Don't rate it; personally, our lot usually steers clear of outside criminal interests. Still, he's worth a look. Pity he was alerted, really."

A mild but pointed comment. Superintendent Fumery stiffened

130

perceptibly. "We have our own inquiries to pursue," he said. "In view of the Grover situation, we had to have him in."

All policemen in forces beyond the Metropolitan Area are quick to bristle at any implied criticism offered by visiting men from London. Pete spoke up. "He's not on your lists. I'd suggest that if we hadn't pulled him, you wouldn't have known he exists."

"True. True," said Fowler. "I don't somehow think we'd have missed him much, but there it is. And you've got a tail on him. We'll put one of our lads in with 'em just in case he's chinning with a load of Paddys who they wouldn't recognize. Not that he will, of course. Not now. If he's got your Grover, I don't give much for his chances now. Mind you, if our little friends have got him, you can kiss him farewell for sure, if you're that way inclined." He looked at Pete. "They tell me he's a friend of yours."

"Uh-huh." No denying it; except that if trafficking with terrorists was involved, you could well and truly use the past tense.

"Well, I've got a few peculiar friends myself," the man from London said.

The Chief Constable was no fool. He had good men here tired and edgy from a long day of toil and frustration. Let them get to loggerheads, teamwork must automatically suffer. "Gentlemen," he said, "it's getting late. I suggest we adjourn until the morning, there is nothing we can do for now."

So they broke it up. Fowler and Figge went across to their hotel, the policemen drove to the homes where their long-suffering wives sat killing the solitary hours with telly; and before he had time for the first sip of cocoa, Pete Parsons' telephone rang. It was bound to be for him, probably summoning him back to work. "I'll take it," he said.

It was Charlie. To soothe Sally, who had worked herself up into a very fair state, and to tackle with positive action his own unease, he had tried already to ring Pete at the station, three times during the evening. The first time they said he was still

131

out. The second time they said he was in conference. The third time they said he'd gone home. Time one and time two, he could well have been dodging, nursing wrath. Sally said he was. So ring him at home, to force the issue. Suzie wouldn't let him say he was out, if he was there. She would have seen the paper, too, and if Pete had confided in her, she might be equally mad. Suzie, mad, could not dissemble. Wherefore, here was Charlie now, phone to his reluctant ear.

"Hallo—Pete? Ah. Charlie. I've been trying to get hold of you all evening. So has Sally, only she was this afternoon."

"Oh yes?" said Pete. Very coldly. Did not even ask for clarification.

"Yes. About the story. You know."

"Yes?"

"She didn't do it, mate. It wasn't her fault."

Didn't do it? If she didn't do it, who bloody did? "I'd prefer not to discuss it now, if you don't mind." And Pete put the phone down.

In their house, Sally said, "Was it him?"

"Uh-huh. He's hung up on me."

"Try him again."

"I don't think we'd better. We know how he feels—let him calm down a bit."

"I'll kill bloody Harry," she said.

The early start came at 7 A.M., when Pete groped dozily for the extension phone shrilling with sudden maniacal frenzy beside the bed. He said—it is about the only sound not four-lettered a man can summon, jerked like that out of sleep—"Er-ruh?"

"Pete?" It was Billy the Fumer. "Station just called. Run the electric round your chops, our man's come out of it. I'll be calling in for you, your place. Ten minutes." No fret now, with development imminent. Very chipper, never mind the hour.

Ten minutes later he arrived. Eleven minutes later Pete sat beside him in his car, en route for St. Thomas's Hospital, where they found the team of Fowler and Figge, arrived already and waiting for them. "Morning, gents," said Billy the Fumer. "Lovely day again. Shall we go in?"

Mario was propped up in bed in one of the single rooms—the police had arranged his removal from the public ward—with his turban-bandage still on his head. His eyes now were fully focussed, watching the four solid-bodied men as they came in with the ward sister. Beside him sat the guardian constable, who rose to his feet and addressed the Superintendent.

"Morning, sir."

"Morning," said Billy the Fumer. "Wait outside, will you?" And when the policeman was gone, to Mario: "Well, my son, you've kept us hanging about a bit. We're policemen. Your name is Mario Giovanni Androtti?"

"Yes," said Mario. He knew who he was, so that was all right.

"Yes. Well—I believe you can help us with our inquiries." The Superintendent tucked away his weathered ID card. Nobody else bothered to produce one. The ward sister was hovering. "Madam, I must ask you to leave. Perhaps you will have the goodness to close the door behind you."

Your average woman hates to be summarily shut out from high drama coming to climax before her very eyes, and your ward sister resents being told where she may or may not be in her own hospital. She left in rustling fury, and Mario began to talk.

He needed no coaxing. The game he had been playing was lost, and he stood in mortal dread of other players. Highly dangerous players. So dangerous that all he wanted now was a police guard, all round the clock until they locked him away, comparatively safe in some dungeon. When a man has narrowly dodged a savage death after being chased by evil men, he yearns for a dungeon so deep that only the man with the food can get at him. And the food he would like tasted by some responsible person or persons before delivery. After a greater or lesser period of incarceration he sickens for the outside world again; but in his time of initial

133

shock and terror, safe durance under the eyes of screws is what his bowels yearn for. And very loose they were.

So Mario began to talk. This, in summary, is what he told them. It took an hour or more.

When he left Italy (under a cloud with his family for a foolish attempt to siphon a little money away, but he did not feel it necessary to mention this) he went first to Dublin, where during a year's residence he made certain contacts. It was these contacts who arranged, just before the Bovey Tracey raid, for his moving to England, linking him up with Grover.

A shrewd idea: Italians are less liable to attract scrutiny than are Irishmen, after an ammunition heist. If an Italian is already a restaurant manager by honest profession, and the link is made to a man who owns a new restaurant and needs such a manager, here is connection close to ideal.

How Tom Grover became involved with these Irishmen, Mario did not know. For money, obviously; he never seemed to have any ideological interest. When Mario, spurred partly by the hope of putting himself right back in Italy, suggested when he had sounded the ground and found how greedy the man was, that some of the ammunition be diverted to a much more lucrative market, and a man from Naples had paid an unobtrusive visit, he was in like a shot. The Mafia pays very high money for what it wants, and is lavish in offering other inducements. Like a future of secure affluence, for those who please and are proved useful.

The Bovey Tracey raid was a big one, concentrated on gelignite and plastic explosives, with detonators in their separate little boxes—all nicely shaped to fit into empty cardboard cartons and wooden crates, plenty of which accumulate around a restaurant, stamped with innocuous brand names. Mario knew a bit about explosives. Tommy seemed to know a lot, he appeared to be in sole charge and handled it very expertly.

"Where?" Fowler barked.

"Under a shop," said Mario. "In Stoke of Trent. A big cellar." And he gave a full address. "It's a furniture shop," he added; and

134

Figge slipped out of the room. He wasn't away long, there is a public telephone handy, just out in the hall.

The method was simple. Most criminal operations are. Hans was already in residence when Mario arrived, a strong-arm man recruited, the Italian believed, while Grover was in prison; bodyguard for that man, who used him for appearance's sake as driver with his haulage firm and latterly as waiter—part of his bodyguard duties, in fact, since Grover spent most of his evenings at the restaurant. And Hans it was who followed after Grover had been to the shop, to pick up packages he had stowed into pianos and the like and to drive them, with the stripped-out pianos and various other sound instruments, back to the haulage depot in town. Nothing bizarre about the occasional visit of a smallish haulage truck to a piano shop.

There were only eight, nine of such runs spaced through the year, and when they took place Grover saw to it that the haulage depot was cleared of personnel. Not difficult—office staffs go home at five-thirty, drivers can be given short hauls to have them back early and off the premises, those who do not fit into the regular schedules—and Grover, the busy man supervising two businesses personally, made out the schedules. Those left would be on long runs keeping them out all night, or on rest days and so on. And Phillips, the manager, worked office hours when not needed later. The boss saw to it that on these nights he was not needed. No, said Mario, Phillips was not involved. He wasn't really manager, he did none of the booking and scheduling. Transport manager was his true function.

So, on those few nights, Hans would get in to the depot during the evening, with only Tommy there. Nobody takes note of a truck arriving late at a haulage depot; it happens all the time. A wash and a change of clothing and Hans would be off to the restaurant, leaving Tommy working late. He worked late often, quite legitimately. Sometimes he even had the beat policemen in for a drink.

When the restaurant closed, Hans and Mario would go together to collect the Dodge van, left earlier by Mario in a town car-park. Away to the depot, and a quick off-and-on loading job. After which the van would be driven away by Mario, back to its secret garage, with Hans following in his own vehicle, left, as every day, with all the other drivers' cars at the depot. The van stashed, back together in Hans' car.

"Where did Grover keep this van?" Mr. Fumery asked.

"We rented a garage," said Mario, and gave another address.

So that was it; they all went home. Next day or the next, at whatever time Grover instructed, Hans drove the van away and left it in a car-park in the big city. The following morning he collected it again, empty. The pianos went back to the shop.

"What car-park?"

Mario named it, the big all-night park near the city centre. Figge, who was back in the room, left again.

Fowler put a question in. "Who took over the van from there?"

"The IRA," said Mario.

"Names?"

"I don't know."

"Where did they take it?"

"I don't know. He handled all that. Except—"

He went on to tell of the three occasions when loads had been collected and diverted to a different rendezvous point, from whence they travelled by a devious route to Naples. From this rendezvous the van returned with accounts of moneys salted away for them, overseas. And certain packets. The Mafia paid a proportion in drugs. Very lucrative, profit piled upon profit.

"You were taking a helluva chance, weren't you?" Fowler said. "Mucking about with an Irish contract?"

"Mr. Grover thought he could cover it," said Mario. "This was the last consignment, we were to be gone."

"Gone where?"

"I was—to Napoli." With money awaiting, and reinstated to favour, a job well done. "I do not know where Mr. Grover was going. We had—an aeroplane—we were to be flown—Brittany. And then to separate. Hans was going back to Germany."

136

"Instead of which," Fumery said, "you're here, Grover is apparently blown to bits, and your Hans is missing."

Mario looked surprised. "Hans," he said, "was driving the van."

Well, that put them right on one point. With all the main outline blocked in, it remained only to sort out the details, like . . .

Fumery: "You'd better give us the full story, lad, you're in deep enough as it is." A small threatening gesture, and one that Mario might just as well have ignored. He was in so deep, no charge of withholding information would have landed him deeper. "Not very convincing, that a man with two profitable businesses would desert them and fly off with a little capital made from flogging a few loads of explosives."

"From the drugs," Mario said. "The restaurant—it was not profitable—and I think not the other firm."

"How long was he dealing in drugs?"

"I do not know, from before I was sent, I think. I think—I expect—since he was in prison. He would have met—people—there. And the—people—in Italy—they investigate—perhaps they knew—he was to continue to work for them. That was part of the arrangement, the bargain I was instructed to put to him." The offer, if they knew enough about him, that he couldn't refuse.

"Where was he to work for them?" Fowler again. "What doing?"

"I do not know, I am very junior, they do not tell me. Drugs, I expect, somewhere. He was—a useful man—for them."

The case had blown itself enormously, far beyond the town policemen's sphere. But the original inquiry had to be pursued. Fumery said, "The fire-bomb. What do you know about that?"

"Nothing. Nothing." There was sweat, suddenly, on what could be seen of Mario's forehead. "I think—maybe the IRA—found out. Or the other side—the Provos—this is what they do. Isn't it?"

"Or he crossed your boys, too. They don't muck about, do they?"

"I—think—no—it was not them." But he did not sound too sure.

"Why?"

"They would not be so—clumsy. And they would not chase us through those lanes."

"Nobody chased you, lad. You were running away from a bunch of daft young herberts going home from a party. I don't suppose it interests you, but they're all dead."

And this was the first that Mario knew of that aspect. He still did not know—and nobody could tell him, so presumably he never would—how some terrified inner reflex sent him staggering and stunned along the towpath, fleeing from the terrible vengeful men his fear had conjured up; until he got into the sheep pen, presumably seeking by instinct some sort of cover; and there finally collapsed. He remembered nothing of sheep pen or Sally, of Charlie, of the lifting and carrying and the journey in an ambulance. This little part of his life was blank. The brain is indeed a very funny thing. He linked up with his mind again only this morning. One small thing he did now remember.

"But—there was a police car—"

"Does that surprise you, charging through the country on a Sunday? Again it won't interest you, but you blinded one of our boys."

No, Mario was not interested. All his interest was fixed upon himself. Pete Parsons put a question. "What about this protection gang—could they have put the bomb in?"

"There wasn't a protection gang," Mario said. "I think Mr. Grover knew it was—them. The other people—he was afraid you—the police—would find out about the—business. I think he think he can make you look another way. He made up the protection gang, I think."

"But you said you saw them. In the restaurant."

138

"He telephoned me, told me what to say. I did not know what was happening."

Nor did he, by the sound of it, Pete thought. How *could* he be—how *could* cricket-playing, happy-happy Tommy Grover— how *could* he be a murderous, truly evil bastard? But it seemed he was, not much doubt about it. He asked another question, knowing the answer.

"Where was—Grover—on the night of the fire?"

"He—we—were dealing with—the last load."

Fowler came in again. "Where were you taking it Sunday, if you didn't know who was waiting for it?"

"I—he had vanished—I thought—we thought—they had burned his house. He left no instructions—I thought he'd ring. But he didn't. We thought they'd—or the police had—I had to get rid of it, I thought we could hide it somewhere—"

"Why not leave it in the garage?"

"We thought—if you were inquiring into him—you would find out about—the garage—the van—and it might not be you. We didn't know—what to do."

"You panicked," said Fowler flatly. "That I can believe. Get it right down, you haven't got a gut between you, you scummy little people. Well, Mr. Fumery—if you don't want him any more. . . ?"

"For the present," said Fumery, "no."

"We'll leave you now, then, boyo. But we'll see you again, never doubt it."

Urgently, face shining with sweat, Mario cried in a voice gone suddenly shrill: "You must guard me—you must not leave me here alone—"

"Don't worry, son," Fowler said. "We won't take our eyes off you until we bury you. And if I had my way, we'd be digging now."

The four big men moved to the door. In the passage outside stood two more men, as big but younger, and scruffy. They must have been whistled up by Figge, to augment the police guard.

Obviously, there were more Special Branch operators in the town than the two who reported in to the station. "Right, fellers, don't lose him," Figge said, as Pete turned at the door to ask a final question.

"Did Mrs. Grover know what was going on?"

"I don't know. She was—she should not have been in the house—and the baby. They were—she should have gone to Chester. I think—maybe—he would have fixed for them to join him. Later." Mario's yellow face crumpled. He was weeping. For himself, no doubt. Surely not for them? But he'd dandled the baby on his knee, and Italians adore children.

Newly returned from the hospital, they sat in the Chief Constable's office—Billy the Fumer, Fowler and Figge, Pete Parsons. The Chief himself was there, come directly from home because he did not want to give the impression, by chasing them to the hospital, that he could not trust these high-ranked and eminently professional men to handle the matter without his breath upon their necks. If he fretted while he waited, that was purely his affair. He may well have done, this case was much bigger than the normal run of business. He was sitting back in his chair now, saying with steepled fingers,

"Well—that may have cleared a little dead wood out of the way. And then again it may not. At least it seems to eliminate the protection gang. But we now add the Mafia."

"And possibly the UDO, or some other bunch of mad Belfast Micks," said Fowler, "if they nosed out that the stuff was being flogged to the IRA."

"So where have we come to?" the Chief asked. A rhetorical question, obviously, since he answered it himself, ticking the points on his fingers. "You, Mr. Fowler, have definite IRA involvement, definite Mafia—"

"Mafia's not for us," Fowler put in. "London'll send another bunch to fiddle about with that; I've been on the blower."

"Possible UDO or similar, and nobody definitely in view to give a lead." The Chief resumed his finger-ticking, politely suspended while the Special Branch man spoke. "For our part, in the case of the man Grover, we have: possible IRA, they having found out he was double-crossing them by selling to the Mafia; possible UDO, or whatever, they having found out he was dealing with the IRA; possible Mafia action, if he was double-dealing with them, too—and he seems capable of it. The man Parry—the man Kelly—quite a formidable list. Quite a tangle, and no real lead in any direction. What do you say, Mr. Fumery?"

"Not much *I* can say, sir," answered Billy the Fumer. "You've said it all. Whoever's got him, I reckon we can count Grover as dead by now."

"More than likely," the Chief said. "But not quite definitely, if one of our private citizens has him."

"As good as," said Billy, "if they've got him tucked away well enough. They're not going near him, that's for sure."

"Parry might. He is, after all, not necessarily bound by rational behaviour. If Parry has him, he might follow the obsession right through, he might act according to his need to gloat—"

"We don't know where Parry is, sir."

"No," said the Chief. "No. That was very unfortunate. We will, of course, catch up with him again, but—" The intercom buzzed on his desk. He leaned forward to flick the switch. "Yes?"

The instrument spoke aloud, like the brisk spirit of a biscuit tin. "Call for Superintendent Fowler, sir."

"Thank you." The Chief raised his eyes to Mr. Fowler. "Will you take it here?" Professional grace. The Special Branch man could say, if he wished, "No—ensconce me in a broom cupboard." This one returned the courtesy, waiving his undoubted right to cloak-and-dagger privacy.

"Thank you, sir."

"Put it through." The Chief picked up one of his two phones and offered it.

"Hallo," said Fowler. "Ah." He picked a ball-point out of his pocket and looked around for something to write on. The Chief pushed a memo pad across the desk. The Special Branch leader was saying, "Uh-huh. Yep. Yes. Uh-huh." He began to make notes on the pad. "Clovis Street. Yep. Give me the car number again. Right. Stay there. What are you in? Mortarboard? Water Board. Thought you said mortarboard. Good. If they come out, don't lose 'em. Radio to here, they'll relay it if I'm out of contact. And keep your heads down." He handed the phone back to the Chief Constable and looked at the memo pad. "SJX 192 Z. Is that your man Grover's car? Blue Rover."

Pete answered. As the one who knew the car best, he was the only one who could swear to it offhand. "Yes." Every kind of shock and upset was in him, and an almost unbelieving revulsion against Tommy; and yet there was something different from the normal hunter's quickening in the sudden punch of his heart. Personal involvement lingered.

"It's in a garage, attached to number 30 Clovis Street. Know it? In the city. My lads traced it out, they've lugged up a man-hole. Had time to nose about a bit. Couldn't do much, they don't know how many are in the house. Garage has got a ventilation grille, they managed to squint through it." Fowler was doing things as he spoke, unbuttoning the jacket of his off-the-peg suit to reveal a shoulder holster, removing the stubby revolver from it, breaking it to check the load. Figge had swung away, leaving the room almost at a run. "If you're coming," Fowler said, "better get shooters, in a hurry."

"Ah," said the Chief Constable. "Will that be necessary?" Of course they were going, to wherever Grover's car was. How could they not? "You appear to be armed—"

"Up to you," Fowler snapped. Nothing deferential about it, he'd even dropped the "sir." "Only we don't know how many are in there. Believe me, if it's our sods, they'll be loaded."

"Ah," the Chief said again. He did not fancy any kind of Kojak-battle. Especially on City Force territory, his men involved. He hesitated. Fowler snapped again, resettling the stubby gun in its holster.

"I'm leaving now."

"Ah," said the Chief. He made the decision. "All right, Mr. Fumery—draw guns, yourself and Mr. Parsons. I'll follow—I must have a word with the city police."

"Don't let 'em come thundering up with the sirens howling," Fowler said. "They can make a right cockup. This one's down to us. Right? Keep 'em well away."

"It's down to us, too, Mr. Fowler." The Chief was snapping now. He had the right, and reason. Superior rank, and the coming home at last of solid material within his area of responsibility. "I would remind you that the car belongs to *our* inquiry."

"Yes—well—we'll argue later. If you're coming, gents, let's have your skates on. I've got two men all alone down there, stuck in a bloody manhole."

11

Women are, of course—or many of them are—most vulnerable to emotional upset during the metabolic disturbance at the start of their courses. Sally was one of the vulnerable. Normally it gave no great trouble—she snapped more readily, at Charlie and in her mind at the whole bloody irritating world; she fretted over her work; she swallowed a few aspirin, sometimes she wept a little. That's about all, it was soon over. But this time was different.

She slept badly, tossing and turning, crying out once in nightmare, starting up with flailing arms. When Charlie shook her awake she wept, clinging to him until she returned to the tossing and turning, grinding her teeth from time to time as stressed children often do.

So Charlie himself had a bad night. Probably would have even had he moved into the guest room, where the hours glided by in silent tranquility. But he wouldn't do that. He loved her. So what with her problem and the troubles in his own mind, he lay with his unravelled sleeve very nearly unknitted, feeling nastily hot and sweaty. And she was giving off heat like a restless little steam kettle. There are times when single beds are a boon.

He was up at seven, leaving her sleeping peacefully at last. He looked out at the day—another scorcher, it was going to be—and showered away the sweat of the night. Shaved, cleaned his teeth, sat down with yesterday's *Evening Courier,* reading again the story that should not have been there. The morning papers, he imagined, had probably taken it up, but he would not know what they said until the delivery boy arrived. He never came before eight.

At seven forty-five he looked at Sally's desk diary. Better get her up, he said to himself, she's got an appointment at nine-thirty. So he made a cup of tea and took it up. When he shook her shoulder she jerked awake and said, "Pete?" So he knew the matter was still troubling her mind.

"I hope not," he said. "There'll be hell to pay if it is."

She did not smile. She said, "Oh—I was dreaming of—oh—lovely—ta." She took the tea. It slopped over. "Bugger it," she said savagely. "Now look what you've made me do."

Oh oh, he thought—another fun-filled day. He said, "Sup it out of the saucer, pretend you're a bus conductor." And he left her there.

She was up and showered and down almost before the bread popped brown from the toaster. He'd put the honey out, it seemed like a morning when she would take honey, with a trifle of fruit juice and not a little hot coffee. A man gets to know these things. He had the coffee bubbling.

This morning she was toying only. Drank the fruit juice, smeared toast with honey, pushed it aside, and went straight on to the coffee. Sitting at the table with her hair pinned back and no makeup, she looked about thirteen, and moody with it. She spread through the bright kitchen the sort of silence that gives echo to thunderous crunching as you work your way through your own toast.

She was still drinking coffee when the morning paper flopped loudly through the letter box. Charlie went to fetch it. He brought it through, scanning for the story. This paper, anyway, did not give front-page treatment, there were better things to think about. Page 3 featured it, more or less recapitulating what appeared in last night's *Courier*. He said,

"Mm—they haven't front-paged it, it's on page three. You ought to give 'em a buzz, tell 'em you want paying space-rate. Half of it looks as if it's lifted from yours."

He offered the paper. She shoved it aside with thirteen-year-old petulance. "I don't want to see it," she said. "I'm sick of the bloody story."

"Well, anyway, Harry was right—the bar was off. They can't have you for it."

"Wish they could," she said. "Not me—him. Bloody Harry." Tears sprang suddenly to her eyes again. She wiped them away with a table napkin.

"Oh, come on now," said Charlie. "It could be worse; it's not all bad—"

"Of course it is." Another tear, another wipe. "With Pete, of course it's bad. What's Suzie going to say?"

"Want me to ring him again?" He hated to see her upset. Except when he did it himself. Even then he didn't like it.

"What's the good of that, he keeps cutting you off. I'm going in to see him."

"When?"

"On the way in to the office."

He'd thought she might. Had wondered, in fact, if he should do it himself. But there was a snag. If Pete was in Dutch already from traffic with them, would it not raise eyebrows, their arriving for a private conference in the thick of it? "I'm not sure you should do that," he said.

She flashed at him. "Well, I'm doing it."

And she would. No use arguing—if she meant to do it, do it she would. "I'll come with you," he said. Better be there. To fight for her if necessary, against Pete and his scorn. Not that she wasn't a bonny fighter, but—well—she was upset. She might even make things worse.

"Please yourself. I don't need anybody holding my hand."

"I'm in it, too, aren't I? Pete's my mate."

She left the table without another word, making for the bathroom, where she spent a considerable time before going up to the bedroom, the dressing table with all those exotic little bottles and boxes, and the pretty stool to sit on while she worked. He did not see her again until nearly nine, by which time he had rung his fat boss, to say that he would be late in. Not that he had to account for every hour of his every day, but he'd left unfinished last night a report the fat man would be screaming for, and which he wouldn't get now until he got it. The fat man said,

"Sod it—if you're coming in late, you might at least stay overnight and clear up."

"Didn't know I was going to be late, last night."

"You buggers seem to think we run the firm for your benefit. And another thing—your funny buddy Grover—bloody good bit of business you brought in there. You seen the bloody papers?"

"Of course I have."

"Bloody IRA—explosives—Christ knows what. I hope you don't expect us to pay out on this lot. Not without extensive investigation."

He was talking a lot of cock. He was talking from needle with Charlie, riled at his coming in late. He was talking because he was a silly, silly fat man, and a fat man being pompous, to boot. "Be your age, Tubso," said Charlie, and hung up. Who expected anybody to pay out? Who were they going to pay out to, anyway? If Tommy was dead—here was a jolly question. He wouldn't be making claims, would he?

When she came down, she was gorgeous. A plain dress in something like linen, which he would have called buff but she probably knew was oatmeal or something; blue shoes, a blue handbag, a blue belt, and her hair all rich and shining. Oh, she'd uncorked her bottles all right, she'd cunningly wielded the eyeliner. Full war-paint this, even to the false lashes that so unnecessarily gilded the lily. A woman knows that perfumed and impeccable sex is her one true weapon, her shield and her buckler in confrontation with sweaty-handed, libido-burdened man. She looked cool. She looked poised. She wafted, every pore a promise of Pasha's paradise. "By God," said Charlie—and he her husband. That says a lot— "You look bloody lovely."

"Why wouldn't I?" she snapped. "I *am* bloody lovely." And she swept past with her head in the air.

He followed her out into the sunshine. As she came from shadowed door into bright sun, the light through the summer dress showed the full length of her moving legs, slimmed by the high heels she wore. Begod, he thought, if old Pete comes up against her in a bit of back lighting, she might not have all that much to worry about. I'm the one with no chance. Old hairy-legs.

She went directly to her own small car, standing in the drive. "Are we taking yours?" he said.

She really was snappy this morning. Not to be wondered at, of course. "I'm not coming back for it, if that's what you mean. I've got a job at half past nine."

Oh well—he wasn't going to fight, she'd had a terrible night. He'd get a cab back, collect his car. He climbed into the passenger seat. As she was about to drive away, he asked mildly, "Got your camera?" Knew very well she hadn't.

"Damn," she said, and got out, and went into the house again. She would need her camera. The council was going to bulldoze one of the few lovely eighteenth-century houses left still unmolested in the town. She was to meet the formidable lady spearheading the Conservation Society protest. She'd need a shot or two, the lady square in tweed and her fore-and-aft hat, with the house as background. No point in taking a photographer along; she usually did her own column pictures.

She came out, slung the camera case onto the back seat, and nosed the car through the gate. They travelled in silence into town. He thought: We'll best use the CID door. If we go in through the front, there may be a clutch of pressmen. And Reception will ring through; if Pete says he's out, that's it. The other way, we may beard him before he knows we're there—and with a little bit of luck, unseen. As they approached the station, he said, "Better use the CID door."

"I was going to. Do you think I'm stupid?"

A loaded question. Many a man has had his skull bent for answering that one.

Guns were issued and signed for, the cumbersome .38 Webleys still good enough in areas where the gun-toting policeman is very, very rare indeed. Both Billy the Fumer and Pete Parsons had toted before, no police career entirely escapes call-out to some berk with a gun; but neither had been called upon to squeeze a trigger, except on the practise range, where they had put many a round into and about the belly of a mad-looking dummy that went *twang-g-g-g* when you hit it.

Both the local men had hurriedly donned the jackets hung on pegs in their offices when they returned from the hospital, to hide the shoulder holsters that felt lumpy and heavy against the side ribs. Mr. Fumery said to Mr. Fowler, as they went down the stairs,

"Your men. Are they armed?"

"Rifles and automatics," said Fowler. "Let's hope they don't have to use them."

"They won't, if it's one of our two." Neither Parry nor Kelly had been known to carry arms. Apart from Kelly's fire-raising activities and a fist-and-boot fracas when Parry was removed into hospital, neither had a history of violence.

"You never know," Fowler said. "And it won't be your two. We've had the house on our list for a long time."

Fumery's reply carried a barb. "Surprising that you didn't get to it sooner. Surprising your men can't tell us who's in there."

Fowler rose to the tone. He snapped: "We've got a lot of suspect houses, not enough manpower. This is a suspect house, not a known one. And nobody's gone in or out since my lads got there this morning."

Actually, the Branch had done very well, to have come up with solid matter in the short time since they were put into the field. Fowler was in no mood to embark on long exposition, so he did not mention that his man, speaking this morning, had asked if he should knock on the house door in his guise of Water Board man, just to tell whoever answered that the flow was about to be cut off. Fowler said no—hold it until I get there. You never can be sure what will happen, when you do a thing like that. Two men might not be enough to handle it.

At the bottom of the stairs they turned left. Not right, which would have brought them out at the front door, via Reception; but left, to the CID door and through onto the roughly flattened open space that would be built over soon, but served now as parking lot for detectives too idle to use the forecourt and walk right round the building, or all the way through to their offices close by the CID door. Figge was out there already, standing by the unmarked car that had brought him and his chief from London. The three men came through the door and hurried toward him just as Sally turned into the road.

There was nothing to obstruct the view from the road across that open ground. Charlie said, "There's Pete—with Billy—who are the others—they're in a hurry—" because Figge had ducked into the driving seat as the others half-ran toward him, and set the car moving almost before they were aboard, Fowler in front and the two local men slammed into the back seat. "They'll be the Special Branch geezers."

The squeal of tyres on loose rubble could not be heard from inside Sally's car, but the slip of rear wheels could be seen, and the urgency behind so swift a take-off was obvious. Charlie felt something very like relief as he said, "Well—that's it, then. We've missed him."

He expected that Sally would bring the car to a halt; but she trod on no brake. Instead, when the car with the policemen in it took to the road and turned away from them, she pressed the accelerator and followed. Charlie spoke again.

"What the hell are you doing, for Christ's sake?"

"Following 'em," she said.

"Don't be daft—what for?"

"It's got to be big, hasn't it? It's got to be Tommy—what'll you bet they've found Tommy?"

He wasn't betting anything. Who bets, when a woman believes she is tuned in to her intuition? So often, you find that she was. But more than intuition was at work in Sally. Pressman's nose was at it, too. And Charlie knew her thinking.

It had to be, his own nose knew, something big, most likely connected with Tommy. And *that* was a scoop, a blinding gift from God come falling out of the blue. Even if it had nothing to do with Tommy, it must be worth having. What—Billy the Fumer, Pete Parsons, and two Special Branch, all leaping aboard and galloping off in every direction? IRA or—something. At least. It was what they'd all been working on. But . . .

She seemed to have forgotten that she came to put things right with Pete, not to complicate the matter. The car ahead was turning onto the main road to the city. As she followed, she chortled, "Ho, ho—this'll stop bloody Harry in his tracks."

"I thought you were finished with Harry." Last night she'd said she was. Last night she was resigning from the paper.

"He's not getting it." The car ahead was travelling in the fast lane, but not so fast as to make her following conspicuous. "Not a sniff; he'll tear his hair out. If this is what I reckon, it goes to the agencies. Or a national exclusive. With a byline. Good thing I brought the camera." She added, "This is the *big* one. *Everybody* will want it."

There really was no time to think the matter through, that was the trouble. And Charlie's own nose by now was urging him on. He might, perhaps, have argued more strongly against it had there been time to consider coolly. As it was, he merely said, "You'll be nicked for speeding if you don't watch it, before you even get there."

"Not on this road," she retorted.

And she was right—permitted speed here was 70 miles per hour. The needle was flickering around it. The police ahead, after the over-keen start, were not risking pile-up, or the delay built in to being stopped by and having to explain to a squad car. They were in contact already with Fowler's two Water Board men, there appeared to be no reason why they should shoot into the city like an attempt on the land speed record.

They were, in fact, almost entering the outer suburbs when Figge, looking into his driving mirror, said, "There's a geezer behind, been there all the way. Think he's following us?"

Billy the Fumer, in the back, craned to see through the rear window. "Doubt it," he said. "It's a fast road. More likely just a commercial traveller, bit behind on his rounds."

The man was paying his last call to Tommy. The last of many, spread through the days; during which he had watched with delight his victim's thirst-torment and swift deterioration, feeding him a sip of water occasionally, just sufficient to keep him from keeling over. More usually he drank what he brought down himself, so that Tommy could see how good it was.

He switched on the light now and came down the unbanistered stairs, carefully because a fall down stone steps can be very nasty. He approached the foetid body huddled on the stinking mattress and stood for a moment grinning down at it, the sadist in his element. Then he kicked it, saying,

"You asleep, then, boyo? Wake up—your dear old friend is here."

The bundle stirred; came from huddling on its side almost onto its back. Tommy's eyes opened. Dying eyes, bloodshot and dazed, sunken into hollowed sockets. The man said,

"Ah. That's my boy. I thought you might have snuffed on me. So: This is it. This is where we put you down. We're away, do you see." His Northern Irish twang was very strong today. Before, it had scarcely shown. From one pocket he was fetching a six-inch metal cylinder, from under his arm a revolver. Screwing the cylinder onto the gun, he carried on talking.

"Have you seen the papers? No, I suppose you haven't." He smiled at his little jest. "You've managed to stir it up a bit. Not quite

152

front page, but it's in all of them. All about you, IRA and everything. Nothing about us—I think we're clear. Personally, I'd stay; I've enjoyed it here, but Belfast says move on. There's a lot of Special Branch activity, the Terrorist Squad's hopping about. I suppose they're right; in Belfast, these bastards can't tell the difference between one Irishman and another. Better safe than sorry.

"Mind you, I can do with a little fresh air. I've been holed up here since I brought you in. You know how trying it can be, all cooped up. Well, we'll both be out of it soon."

He tested the fitting of the silencer on the barrel, slipped off the safety catch, and sat on his stool, holding the gun on one knee. "They say in the papers," he said, "that you disappeared after starting out for Chester. You were going a very funny way to Chester, weren't you? You wouldn't get to Chester on that road."

Perfectly right. The layby where Tommy stopped to ring Mario was hardly clear of the town, on the south side. The only sensible way to Chester was to leave town heading north. The man paused, as though he might get an answer. Huddled and filthy, black-jowled with days of stubble, hollow-eyed, unkempt and waxy, Tommy said nothing. Perhaps by now he couldn't. The man went on,

"On the other hand, it would take you to the airport, wouldn't it? Was that the idea—had you got the wind up? Were you running for it, did our little bomb frighten you?"

Right on target. That was precisely what Tommy set out to do. Shattered, he cut and ran. Didn't mean to, when he rang Mario with his concocted protection-gang story; but that dreadful night in the Woods' house—that broke him. That destroyed him. He fled—and he could have got away with it, on any commercial flight with the help of Wile-U-Wait photo and a visitor's passport (his own burned in the fire) from a post office; because his Chester story meant nobody would wonder about him for time enough. He made the mistake of trying to ring Mario; because if all deliveries were made as promised to the Mafia, they would— he hoped, he prayed—see him right when he appealed from wherever he went. Let them down, and he was entirely on his own—with more implacable enemies.

Well—trying to ring Mario turned out to be the mistake, and here he was. He should never have stopped at all. But he was not thinking well—horrible man though he was, he had loved his wife and daughter. Shocked, he never gave a thought to organisations outside IRA and Mafia.

"Were you making for Ireland?" the man was saying. "Your IRA friends? The bastards—did you think we didn't know? Ah well—you're here now, aren't you? Until I pull my little trigger."

He levelled the revolver. Tommy's eyes widened, he struggled suddenly, mewing, against his bonds. The man laughed, lowered the gun, said as if struck by a happy idea:

"No. Tell you what—do you know the game of Russian roulette? Very simple. I take out the bullets—" He broke the load-cylinder from the gun, shook out the bull-nosed cartridges into his hand. "Now—I put one back. See? Like this. And I spin the cylinder. Now—you don't know where the bullet is. I don't know where the bullet is. Let's find out, shall we?"

Again he levelled the gun, made long-snouted by the addition of the silencer. This time he pulled the trigger, Tommy cowering. The hammer fell with a click.

"There," said the man, very brightly as if playing games with a child. "That wasn't it, was it? Let's try again."

Again the hammer clicked.

"No? Well, well. That's two. It must be one of the other four, mustn't it? Wonder if it's this one."

It was not. The gun clicked again.

"Your luck's in, isn't it? Gives you time to pray. Although I doubt if He'll take much notice. Let's see what happens to you this time."

This time, the gun fired with a soft plop. But oh—the man was expert. At each pull of the trigger he had raised the barrel, almost imperceptibly, so that the bullet now flew a split inch above Tommy's cowering head—the hollow, stretched eyes were

154

weeping now, the face a distorted mask of glistening terror—to bury itself in the wall.

The man laughed. "Changed my mind. Aren't you the lucky one? Too quick. Waste of all the work I've put in." He flicked out the cylinder, removed the spent case and began to pack back in the five live cartridges remaining. Like the good gunman he was, he placed the empty chamber first in the firing order. No disconcerting misfire not allowed for, if you have to meet trouble without time to think. The professional is neat and methodical always. And ready. He talked as he worked.

"What I'm going to do, I'm going to leave you here. I give you two, maybe three more days, all gagged up. I shall enjoy thinking about it, wondering how you're getting along. Pity I can't see the job through to the end, I have enjoyed knowing you. But there it is, we can't have everything, can we?"

He stood up, the silencer unscrewed and returned to his pocket, the revolver back in its shoulder holster. "Good-bye then, Mr. Grover," he said. "I'd wish you luck, but it's all run out on you." He turned away.

Upstairs in the living room, two men waited. Unremarkable men in unremarkable suits. He was himself unremarkable. One of the men said, "Finished?"

"Uh-huh." He'd gone down to the cellar to shoot Tommy. He was not going to tell these men that he had changed his mind, unable to resist this strongly sexual joy in torture. Even now he could feel the hardness, the loin-tingling it always brought him. "Are we ready?" he said.

The same man answered, turning back to the filling of an airline bag open on the table. Two more soft bags stood on the floor. "Couple of minutes. Just got to pack my underwear."

The police had arrived already, in the street outside. Clovis Street led directly off the main road, this side of the city proper; which was fortunate in that it meant no threading through crowded streets. They homed to it accurately, guided by Fowler with the map

155

spread on his knee and the radio channel open to his men in a hole. You can never be sure who is tapping, so they were saying nothing. Which meant: no movement in or around the house.

It was a long street moving towards moribund, small shops forced out of business by supermarkets interspersed with lone houses too big for today's mini-families, who live by choice in breeze-block tiddlywink containers. Long enough, it was, for Figge to note the second car turning in off the main road, a full two hundred yards behind. "That bugger *must* be following," he said.

Fowler's concentration was fixed ahead, where a Water Board van stood at the curb. In the middle of the road nearby, wooden barrier-hurdles had been erected around a manhole cover, raised to form a shield between two shops, only one open for the sale of the small groceries women forget when they shop in the city. The glum proprietor survived on Oxo cubes, tins of beans, and Saxa salt.

Both rear-seat passengers twisted to see. The unaccountable car was too far away for the number plate to be distinguishable, or for the occupants to be recognized; but Pete, who had seen it often enough, thought with alarm: That looks like Sally Wood's car. Oh Christ—no. No.

Billy the Fumer spoke to Figge; curtly, because tension mounts in armed policemen as they close with they don't know what. "Nothing to do with us." He added, "Keep an eye on it, Pete."

They were passing a crossroad formed by two tributary streets. At a discreet distance back on one side stood two blue-and-white police cars, empty but for the drivers. On the other was a personnel carrier, very neatly parked and also containing only the driver. The Chief Constable, on his way by now from the station, had used telephone and radio to good effect before he set out. These would be City Force men, gone out of sight as big policemen surprisingly can do without being noticed at all. There would be others, somewhere beyond the house. The orthodox boxing in.

"Don't crowd it," Fowler said. "Stop this side of the house." Without a grunt Figge steered the car in, bringing it gently to rest. Sally, just passing the minor crossroads, noted the evidence there and said, "See? Something's up."

Charlie, too, had seen the police transport. "We ought to get out of this," he said uneasily. "Drive straight on, go home."

"What, now?" she said. "You're joking."

He wasn't, begod. What, at a time like this? But he'd known she wouldn't tamely pack up and go now, with the scoop of a lifetime dangling right before her nose. Professional she was, let no one doubt it. But Pete wouldn't like it. Better stay away from Pete.

"If you're stopping, then," he said, "don't go right in behind them." He was, remember, a policeman. Go in close, jump out grinning inanely—you not only anger Pete, you are a civilian liability appeared in the thick of it, whatever it may be, and you can alert quarry to too much unusual activity happening beyond the curtains. "Stay fifty yards short of 'em. On the opposite side." Sally swung the car over.

The policemen did not come out from their car. Four big men materialised for no obvious reason, with nowhere definite to go and the indefinable something about them that cried "copper" to the experienced bent, is bad news. They certainly could not stroll along for a chat with the Water Board men. So they stayed, while Fowler broke radio silence. "Bunny?" he said, into his little microphone.

"Uh-huh," the set replied. Immediate, but noncommittal.

"You in burrow?"

"Uh-huh. Doe's in hutch."

"Other bunnies?"

"Don't know."

There would be others, of course. There were alleyways, there were empty shops offering good field of fire to the house. No doubt about which house, the angle of the manhole cover was guide enough, positioned as shield against it. And as pointer to it. A good bunny, in that hole. The city lads were performing well, too, if they were already in position. You could see no hide or hair of them.

Neither of the Special Branch men explained the code, nor did the town policemen need it. The burrow had to be the hole, hutch the Water Board van. One bunny in each. Covering from two positions, without hampering each other as they would if both were cramped into the hole. The bunny in the hutch, too, would be handling the longer-range radio set used to maintain contact on the journey from town. The man who just spoke would have been using his walkie-talkie.

Pete Parsons, twisted to keep an eye on the extraneous car as bidden, saw it pull across the street and stop at the opposite curb, fifty yards away from the police car, about a hundred from the house. He knew now who was in it, and four-letter words went steaming through his mind. Aloud, he said nothing. Billy the Fumer craned round to look. Billy wouldn't have known whose car it was had it run over his foot. "What does that bugger think he's doing?" he said.

Figge glanced briefly, catching the reflection in his wing mirror. "Some more of 'em?"

Fowler said, "Could be. If they are, they've run their noses in—if your lads are on the job, matie there's sitting right under the guns."

They were not Billy's lads. They were City lads, and Billy didn't know how they were deployed. But yes—they were probably in that empty shop almost opposite where the car had stopped. A couple of guns would be keeping it under obbo, just in case.

"They might have a radio," Figge said. "Our herberts may have scarpered already, out the back way."

"Back'll be covered," said Fowler, "if our heroes know their kit. And if they were gone, the car wouldn't stop. Might be here to pick 'em up."

Billy's face screwed into an irritated frown. "One of 'em looks like a woman."

"Er—" said Pete. "I think it's—er—it *could* be Sally Wood."

158

"Sally bloody Wood?" the Super exploded. Nerves. Pure nerves. "The *Courier* bird? The girl you leaked the IRA lark to? You didn't—?"

Pete's nerves, too, were twanging catgut. "Course I bloody didn't," he snarled. It jolted him badly, Billy's bald revelation that he knew where the leak had come from. He should have known—did know, in his heart—that Billy would put two and two together. Detective's speciality.

"What the bloody hell is she doing here, then?" barked Billy the Fumer.

Pete barked back. "How the bloody hell do I know?" The Special Branch men glanced at each other with raised eyebrows.

Sally was, in fact, unscrewing the short-range lens from her camera and putting it in her lap while she fetched the telephoto lens out from the case. As she screwed it home, Charlie said flatly, "You're not getting out of the car."

"Won't need to, will I? I can shoot from here." Her tone, too, was snappy. There was a lot of nervous tension around that street. She put the discarded lens carefully into its wash-leather bag and stowed it as carefully in the proper compartment. Expensive items, lenses, and this was her own paid-for-herself property. She sat with the camera in her lap, looking alertly around; fully engaged now, detached from all but the job in hand. "Come on, come on," she muttered impatiently, entirely to herself. "Let's be having some action."

Charlie, too, was not dozing off. He had the salient house pinpointed—it had to be that one, the only one between the policemen's car and the Water Board van. And that van—and the hole with its shielding cover up—coppers. He was also guessing now that the shop almost opposite, just slightly back from where he sat, held more coppers. He couldn't see any; but that's where he would have put some, with more on the far side of the house. The policemen were not getting out of the car. He didn't expect them to. He said, "We're bloody crazy, being here. Could be hours before anything happens. *If* anything happens."

159

"It'll have to be hours, then, won't it?" Sally snapped. Back in the town a lady fumed for her, standing in front of a Georgian building in her fore-and-aft hat.

"You think this is putting you right with Pete?" Putting us right, he could have said.

But she was sitting bolt upright. "Look—he's coming out of his hole."

From that hole in the ground a head was rising, followed by shoulders, a trunk, arms that braced on the brink while the legs were brought to where the whole man could emerge, to lever himself upright and walk with no discernible trepidation toward the house.

Fowler had conjured him. When he had sat for long enough to have every visible aspect of the situation annotated in his mind, Figge doing the same alongside and Billy fuming beside the silent Pete Parsons in the back, he spoke into his little microphone.

"Want to give it a go, then?"

"Check," said the set; and after no more than the second or two it takes to lay aside a personal radio, up came the bunny's head, all in his Water Board cap.

Now this was the sensible move. Old as the hills, yes. Done countless times, over the years—Water Board, Electricity Board, Gas Board, man come to read the meters— But very effective, so why seek the new and clever? That way lies trouble, and trouble enough we come to in this imperfect world.

True, a Water Board man come to warn that the supply is about to be cut off will not necessarily walk away knowing how many souls are in the house. But he can establish that the somebody who answers the door is there, and maybe who it is. A good, trained eye can often pick up indications of other presences, once the door is opened—coats on hall stands, hats on hooks, various bits. And if nobody answers, very cautious entry by front and rear, after the initial man's withdrawal, will often tell you that you can all pack up and go home. The buggers have gone, or were never there.

So out of his hole came the brave Water Board man. And it is a brave act, to walk up and knock on the door. You don't know who has been watching, who has everything sorted out behind the curtains. You don't know if somebody in there will start shooting now, and you right out in the open. You don't know if you will be snatched in, and used as hostage. Or as shield if they break for it, the stub of a gun in your back. Credit, then, to the Water Board man, out of his hole and walking toward the steps leading up to a green paint-flaking front door. No gates, these houses, no front gardens. Three cast-iron-banistered steps and a line of area railings.

Inside the house, the man at the table had put the last of his underwear into his bag and zipped it shut. "Right," he said.

"Let's go, then," said the man with the revolver under his jacket.

"Got the tickets?" the third man asked. Reasonably, they do get left on mantelpieces.

"Course I've got the bloody tickets." Train and boat, all the way in to Belfast.

"Only asking," said the third man.

Carrying a bag each, they walked along the short passage and opened the front door. Blinking there in the blazing sunshine, one foot raised to mount the first step, was the Water Board man. He lowered the foot to ground level and said, "Ah. How do. I'm afraid I'm going to have to cut your water off." So might a doctor prescribe major surgery.

"Oh. Yes. Right," said the man with the gun under his arm. "Do you have to—er—go into the house? I mean—we're just going out."

The Water Board man could now say yes, or he could say no. To say yes—and he was brave enough—would let him assess whether anybody else lurked within. But the man who spoke didn't know water. Somebody in there might very well know that you turn it off, if you are working on a fault in the main supply, with a thing like a big sardine-can key, out there in the road. So he said, "No. No, that won't be necessary." Because his brief was to knock, not to cock everything up by offering himself as hostage, or at least alerting the subject to something out of kilter. He heard the Irish accent—he'd expected Southern, but Northern can be as deadly—and thought: Provos. The mother-in-law's life on it.

"Right, then." The man with the gun, the two who might be carrying others, stood on the top step still, and the man's eyes were scanning up and down the street. Habit, no doubt, professional guns—and that's what he was, a true professional—stay alive by meticulous concentration on doing so.

Perhaps it was one of Fowler's few mistakes, his getting out of the car. Although, come to consider it, he could hardly let the men walk away. If they were to be taken, here was the place to do it, where they were boxed in by unseen guns. Here, too, most of the buildings looked empty. Farther along they were occupied, and you don't want to mix civilians in with possible mayhem. Why the hell, London will ask if one of them gets shot, didn't you confine the men to the house?

And he recognized that man, do you see. The heavy moustache was gone, but there was no mistaking the beaky nose, the heavy jaw, the black curly hair growing low over the domed forehead. "Sean McBride," he—well, he ejaculated; and began to get out of the car.

Figge also began to move out. He, too, recognized the man when the name was spoken, from photos on file, from obbo through binoculars—Special Branch does a lot of that, the subject never knowing. Fowler's exclamation merely confirmed identity.

The very local men started at the name. Policemen read newspapers, and this man had gunned himself into a measure of fame. His picture, his details were on file at their own station, as a professional gun who side-lined in training groups to kill. So when the front doors opened and the Special Branch men angled to avoid bumping their heads, they too reached for the handles.

162

This may have been the mistake; Fowler, perhaps, should have told everybody else to stay put. He had, after all, plenty of firepower in support, even if he did not know where it was. But hindsight is all very well. And it probably would not have made a lot of difference.

He got out; and he cried: "Hold it there, McBride."

The effect was dramatic. Three bags flopped on the steps and two men collided, as one tried to dodge back into the house and the other to leap down to street level. Amateurs, these. Before they were sorted out, the Water Board man had his gun on them, saying, "All right—all right." They raised quivering hands.

But the pro had reacted. Good job the Water Board man did not jump into his path to stop him, he would have undoubtedly got himself shot. The scanning eyes swung at the cry, the alerted brain gathered flashes: one big man out, one almost out, two coming out of the car. Before his bag properly settled on the steps, his revolver was out and he was off.

The Water Board man let him go. Only way to stop him was with a bullet; and the law will flay the policeman who fires before being fired upon. Especially now he could not fire—somebody was getting out of that car parked on this side, right in the line of fire. Might be more coppers in it, for all he knew. Let them take care of chummy. He concentrated on the two he'd got.

Nobody at all fired, as McBride took wing, partly because of that law, partly because of the girl emerging from that car.

Charlie was trying to restrain her; but he'd grabbed too late. She wrenched away from his clutch and was out on the pavement, levelling that long camera; because what a scoop this would be—the villains in the very act of being arrested.

She did not at first realize that the man was racing this way, and he probably wouldn't have been had the Water Board man not been blocking the other. This way, he had to pass the car and the four men, on the other side of the street. Committed, gun in hand, he ran like the clappers.

When Sally moved, they were all standing on the steps. By the time she had the situation clarified in the viewfinder, it was too late. The man was closing; Fowler was shouting, "Don't be a bloody fool, McBride;" Figge, Pete, and Billy the Fumer all had their guns out but could not use them; and all around, fingers held back from second pressure for the same reasons: The bastard hadn't fired, and the bird was in the way.

There was that open-for-business shop in the way, too. A sudden hail of bullets shattering the window and bouncing off baked-bean cans would aggravate no end whoever was in there. Especially if one buried itself in his head.

When the man raised his gun to Sally, he may have intended, being a compulsive killer, to blast aside the human obstacle in his path. Most likely, he saw her as a lady plainclothes police officer, and the long-snouted camera pointed at him as a weapon of some sort—a new-pattern rifle, something. The man who lives by guns thinks in terms of guns, when he has no time to spare. He raised his revolver; and three things happened, very nearly simultaneously. It was all moving very fast, you must understand.

Charlie sobbed, "Christ! Oh Christ!" and came out from the car—he already had the door open and was on his way—lurching heart loving her, blood beyond thought knowing how much he loved her, his wife with the gun bearing down on her. Enough to die, if it kept her from dying. Greater love hath no man, that he lay down his life for his wife. And the man pulled the trigger, long before Charlie could superimpose himself.

For the only time in his life, sheer professionalism let McBride down. He had positioned that empty chamber first in the order, and all he got now—surprise to him, because what with one thing and another he had forgotten—was a click. Before his finger could tighten again, the other two things happened.

Charlie's head rose as he came upright. And in that empty shop a very young policeman—they get younger and younger—applied second pressure to his rifle trigger without even meaning to. One of several in there, detailed to keep that car covered, fresh-faced, baby-blue-eyed and highly excited by this, his first time under arms, he saw the man on whom he had just beaded click his pistol, and his own gun went off. Just like that. The reflexes of youth are springy, and the titterings of Fate unpredictable.

He got two, with one bullet. Charlie's head came up—ah, it wasn't the poor lad's fault—just as the report sounded. Only shot fired.

Charlie, poising to leap forward, went down on his face, a wallop and a huddle in the road; as a little hole appeared in the chest of McBride, who dropped his gun, clutched at the hole, and fell sideways, to slump down the railings of the adjacent house, while Sally stood—and the four policemen stood—in the absolute silence that followed the shot, bewildered and uncomprehending with the camera coming down from her startled eye.

Then, again, everything started at once. Inside the shop, the young policeman said, "Oh Jesus"; Sally moved; almost hurdling the dying McBride—so self-centred is love, hardly seeing him in her rush to Charlie; throwing away the expensive camera; kneeling in the road, never mind the nylons; cradling his head, his blood all over her nice oatmeal dress; screaming high and loudly, over and over again.

"Oh God, he's dead—he's dead—he's dead—he's dead. Oh God—he's dead—he's dead."

And the four policemen moved, guns out now, headed for the action. Fumery, Fowler, and Figge at the alertly controlled trot policemen do so well—they believed, at this juncture, that others might be in the house. When they went in, of course, they found only Tommy Grover; Pete Parsons streaking ahead, snarling as he went, "You stupid bitch—you stupid, stupid bitch—bitch—bitch—bitch—"

"Stay where you are, you bastards," said the Water Board man to his two men on the steps. Needlessly, they weren't thinking of going anywhere.

12

It was three days later, when Pete Parsons set out at last for a meeting with the Woods. Three days during which a great deal had happened.

On the first, Charlie could not be seen anyway. Removed to hospital, Sally weeping in the ambulance, he lay for the greater part of it unconscious, with a groove in his skull. It didn't need the doctor to confirm that he was so lucky not to be dead. They sedated Sally, too, after he awoke and was pronounced out of danger, so that she was in no condition to be visited, even had he made time; which he did not, and could not. Very hectic day, that was.

The second was as hectic, and scarred by an interview with Billy the Fumer that did nothing to reconcile his mind towards them. Torn between concern, especially for Charlie, so long best friend—damn it, very nearly brother—and deep sorrow, deeper than self-concern and resentment, at the betrayal, he spent another crowded day; during which she tried to phone him several times. He said he was out; while the media made a heroine out of her.

Harry did that, really. Her discarded camera, picked up later, was returned by the police to the office. They thought it belonged there. Harry, having the outline story, tried frantically all day long to contact her, even rushing personally to the hospital. She, hating him and half hysterical over Charlie, would have nothing to do with him. So he had the film developed. Something might be on it.

Something was. She'd clicked the shutter in that traumatic moment, quite involuntarily, twitch of reaction when she realized what was happening. There he was, the murderous Sean Mc-Bride, racing at the camera with gun levelled. Sensational. A second later, he was dead. And our intrepid reporter a girl, no less, and a pretty, lust-worthy one. Sexy-looking husband, too, with a bullet in his nut. Ho ho ho. He'd fixed deals with the dailies, the weeklies, the agencies, the foreign press—for which she would draw the money—before the print was fixed.

So Sally was the nation's little heroine, with Charlie as her heroic Prince Charming; and all through the next day, she tried to ring Pete. She left a final message, in the early evening. "Please," she said, "ask him to meet us. Seven o'clock—or whatever time he likes. Anywhere. Anywhere he chooses. Tell him Charlie's all right, sends his regards."

By now, Pete had telephoned Harry, partly to strengthen his own position. He did it during his chat with Billy, this man sharing the conversation via the extension phone. Not a bad lad at heart, the editor. When he fully realized where he had landed her, he did everything he could to fish her out. Entirely his fault, he said. Misunderstood her—she was most adamant—yes—she seemed determined to resign over it— He even submitted humbly to a dressing down from Billy, and apologized again before they parted. Well, of course, he could afford to be generous. Look what he was sitting amongst.

So Pete had the switchboard ring the Woods' home, to say he would visit them there. Seven o'clock. As his plump and comely Suzie said, he had to see them some time, and she for one never believed Sally meant to do it. Certainly, Charlie didn't. "Go and see them," she said. "Maybe you'll come back in a better temper."

Right on time he climbed out of his car in their drive. Yet another beautiful evening, but the farmers were beginning to make moan as piteously as they did last year, when it rained all the time. Only the ruin next door marred a flower-scented evening, the blossoms hardly wagging in the bee-dozy air-stir. You could hardly call it a breeze.

Sally opened the door before he reached it. For sure she had been hovering, all her lilies gilded. By heck, he thought: Of all the birds old Charlie laid, he certainly picked the pick. Even as he kept the stern set against her of his mind, his libido reached out to fondle her. It often did, as Charlie's fondled Suzie. No good talking, the standing libido has no conscience.

"Hallo, Pete," she said. Awkwardly, with great, grave eyes.

"Hallo, Sally." Not Sal. Sal was too intimate, too much an expression of trust and affection.

"I'm glad you— Charlie's in the living room."

"Uh-huh. How is he?"

"Well—he's home. They said he should stay in, but he wouldn't. Come—er—through."

Charlie was already standing, risen out of his armchair. He wore a turban of white bandage and the over-bright smile that does not sit easy. "Well, well, well," he said. "Old Pete Parsons as ever was. Drink?" He began to move to the liquor cupboard.

"No," said Pete. "Thanks. Just had dinner."

This early? And having had dinner is no reason for turning down a drink. "Oh," Charlie said. "I think I will. Sally?"

"No. And you're not supposed—"

"Only a beer. Sit down, Pete. Sure won't have one? Right." He poured his beer. Pete remained standing. They all did. "Glad you—er—came in. How's Tommy?"

"Fine." They'd dealt with the dehydration, fed him a little soup, and he was talking. What he was saying was proving very useful. He would be going inside for a long, long time, and Mario with him. But Pete was not here to hand out any more gift packages.

"Good," said Charlie. "That is—I mean, good work. Good bit of work, your nobbling him. And the others. Bastard. And Mario. Still can't believe it, really. I thought—that is I—we—wanted to see you because— She—Sally, that is—didn't do it, you know."

"Harry—" Sally put in.

"Uh-huh." Pete was not making it easy for them. They—or she—had not made it easy for him. Not their doing, the one piece of luck: So much pleasure about, so many kudos attaching to the elimination of McBride, the recovery of Grover, so much activity sparked by his ready grassing, that High Authority had no time, and no particular inclination, to probe further a small and, as it turned out, unharmful security leak. But Billy knew. It would go no further; Billy had said so. But had Pete been a small constable, a sergeant, instead of a respected and—hitherto—impeccably trustworthy chief inspector . . .

Charlie's smile grew impossibly brighter. "He blew it; Harry did. She played it exactly as you said. He—well. Anyway—no real harm was done, was it?"

Now Pete spoke. There was none of the old ease of contact about, his tone was quite biting. "That's not the point, is it? A great deal of harm could have been done; you were lucky Special Branch happened to take off the bar." So was I, by Christ. "The point is, there was a leak. And it emanated from here."

Sally opened her mouth. Charlie got there first. "Not by design. Not deliberately."

"Uh-huh." Pete nodded, unsmiling. "That, I am prepared to accept. Let's just call it dangerous negligence, shall we, for a reporter to trust an editor with a written story that should have been kept close secret between her and her source until it was officially cleared."

"Are you sure," said Charlie, "you won't have a drink?"

"No, thanks. I'll be going. Lot of work to do." He turned, and was moving towards the door.

"Ah," said Charlie. "I'll—er—see you out." He spilled a little beer, setting the glass down. Better not have Sally do it. She might burst into tears on the doorstep, or move to shrill, agonized defensive attack. You never quite know what an unhappy woman will do.

The two men passed out through the hall. On the doorstep,

Charlie said, "Well—I'm sorry you . . . Thanks for coming, anyway. Playing Saturday?"

"Depends on work."

"We can use you, without Grover. And I'm out. Well—may see you there, huh?"

"Maybe," said Pete. "Maybe." And he walked away to his car.

When Charlie got back to the living room, she was sitting in her black velvet slacks and gold-white top upright on the extreme edge of her armchair. The stress of these last days showed very plainly on her now, fining down her face, giving a sort of luminous greatness to eyes smudged underneath with pale violet. He said, brightly, "Well—here comes Pete, there goes Pete. Didn't take long, did it?"

She burst—he'd thought she would—into tears. "Oh, Charlie," she wept, "I've been such a fool, I've been such a fool."

"Come on," he said, "you'll be all right. It'll all come right; I know old Pete, he'll get over it."

"I nearly got you killed—I nearly got you—oh—I've been such a fool. . . ."

Even in this day of awkward knees and elbows, a man given sufficient motivation and taken away from self-awareness can still achieve grace. He knelt on the carpet before her, took her in his arms. Her head came down to his shoulder, the loud, distressful tears wetting his skin already through the thin shirt. He patted her back gently, murmuring into her hair.

"There, there, there. There, there, my love—there, there."